I0650377

Percival Pickering

A Life Awry

A Novel: Vol. I.

Percival Pickering

A Life Awry
A Novel: Vol. I.

ISBN/EAN: 9783337047245

Printed in Europe, USA, Canada, Australia, Japan

Cover: Foto ©Andreas Hilbeck / pixelio.de

More available books at **www.hansebooks.com**

A
LIFE
AWRY

"What need to strive with a life awry?"

E. BROWNING.

"Possess thyself, and be content.
Life's best is bound not by the utterance
Of any word, nor may in sound be spent,
To win back echoes out of hollow chance.
What thou hast *felt* is thine.   If much, rejoice."

OWEN MEREDITH.

A
LIFE
AWRY

A Novel

By

PERCIVAL PICKERING

In Three Volumes

Volume I

LONDON
BLISS, SANDS & FOSTER
CRAVEN STREET, STRAND
1893

"It is impossible almost to formulate in words the full mystery of this highest love, which, in its grandest manifestation, only genius gives, and only genius can worthily appreciate . . . for love in its highest meaning is aspiration, the instinct of ascension towards the Divine.

"This homage rendered to another—this life lavished without dream or hope of recompense—this worship given freely and disinterestedly as to a god—is the true essence of womanhood."

"How ridiculous, and what a stranger is he, who is surprised at anything which happens in life!"— M. AURELIUS ANTONINUS.

A LIFE AWRY.

CHAPTER I.

A DRIVING storm of rain was falling. Sweeping far away to the distant hills, it drifted like silver spray over the country, moistening the yellow corn as it passed, washing the dusty hedgerows till their leaves grew clear and glistened. The pale grey soil of the morning was changed to a dull rich brown; here and there in the cart-ruts lay dingy puddles, into which the big splashing drops fell with boisterous vigour.

Along the high-road a dog-cart came swiftly, whirling in and out of the spongy ruts and scattering the embryo puddles right and left. A shower of mud-pellets marked its course, dancing gaily round the quickly-revolving wheels, and starting obliquely from beneath the horse's hoofs; till, spurting thus ever higher and higher, they bespattered the polished surface of the cart, and the two men seated within it drew the mackintosh rug closely about them, in order to protect themselves alike from the moisture descending from the heavens, and from the less cleanly moisture arising from mother-earth.

Since the privilege of a novelist extends to describing the minutest thoughts of persons whose inner self, in real existence, he would be at a loss to unravel; and since the life which has been woven into the following tale is there portrayed by the light of an after-knowledge, which, all-sufficient for those to whom its features were familiar, yet required fanciful touches of light and shade to represent it as faithfully to the eye of a stranger;—since these facts are so, it may be well to explain something

of the reflections and emotions of the two occu-
pants of the dog-cart at this moment when
they were being borne homewards through the
discomfort of a chill summer shower.

The groom who was driving may be briefly
dismissed. The emotional side of his nature
had undoubtedly found employment in inwardly
execrating the little stream of water which,
flowing from his hat, trickled with spasmodic
jerks down his itching nose. His mental
faculties were as unquestionably intent on the
all-absorbing consideration whether—the state
of the heavens being thus unsettled on this
Saturday evening—it might not be equally
unpropitious on the following Sabbath, and, if
this were so, whether an unfortunate predi-
lection for assisting at Divine Worship would
not lead the 'fam'ly' into requiring the
carriage to take them to church. Under these
circumstances, instead of spending a pleasant
morning lying on the grass in some out-of-the-
way nook in the park, basking in the sun and
smoking, he would be compelled to don his

stiff livery and drive two miles — perchance
in heavy rain, to attend a long service in the
stuffy village church, and to get home late for
his dinner, with the prospect of having the
muddy carriage to clean afterwards. A tanta-
lizing fate compared with the lazy, sunny
morning on the grass! Youth, health, summer,
and sunshine are but fleeting treasures; when,
on rare glad days, they lie—all—within our
grasp, it is hard if an untoward chance should
still deny them to us. What wonder if
Higgins felt distinctly ruffled at the possibility?

His companion in present discomfort was
experiencing emotions of a more complex nature,
and revolving problems of deeper interest in
his busy brain. He was a man of about
thirty; a bronzed, stalwart type of Englishman,
with that undefinable spruceness in his general
appearance which the army develops in most
men, but in which there is nothing either
effeminate or foppish. His face, studied closely,
was in irreproachable harmony with the rest
of his person. It was a clean, healthy phy-

siognomy, with as genial and frank an expression as can reasonably be expected in a man who has seen a fair amount of life, and has learnt that his casual self must never, even in trifles, be too unreservedly and naïvely exposed to view.

Yet it was the face of a man who has reached an age when the circumstances of his past, and the mark those circumstances have made in secret upon his soul, must find some distinct expression in his countenance; the mouldings, therefore, of his inner being could by now be traced upon his face, and this was a study in which all might indulge without fear of making any new or startling discoveries in human nature, and one whose counterpart might be perused daily in other men of the same age and class. An average amount of harmless conceit and self-satisfaction might be read there; a truly British tendency to reserve and distrust of the unproven; the impress of some sins which had not been premeditated, and which, when in due course regretted, were not dwelt

upon with morbid sentimentality; a few strongly
pronounced and, perchance, narrow - minded
views on the subject of truth and honour ; and,
above all, an unbounded belief in the time-
honoured creed of Man, that an all-wise Providence cannot dream of demanding the amount
of excellence in him which is, naturally, exacted
to the last farthing in Woman, but has granted
a species of recognized dispensation for all sins
which cannot be classed under the damning
clause of caddishness. In short, unless Captain
Lilcot's face belied him, he was, to all intents, a
very fair specimen of a gentleman; of a man
who is not troubled with an uncomfortable
amount of individuality either for good or for
evil ; of a man with no pretensions to being a
saint, and scarcely more, as the world goes, to
being classified as a sinner ; but who was that
pleasant, and, it may be, wholesome mixture of
the two, so often and so graphically described
as a ' real good sort.'

At the present moment his face betrayed
little or nothing of the tumult of conflicting

emotions which he was experiencing. Mingled
feelings of pleasure and sadness were struggling
for mastery within him, and, while outwardly
calm and impassive, he was undergoing a
variety of sensations to which his placid nature
was wholly unaccustomed.

Trivial as it may appear, foremost amongst
these was an overwhelming delight in the
peace and freshness of the country. After
a long wearying journey from India, followed
by a week of perpetual unrest in London, the
stillness and calm of his present surroundings
produced in him a sense of keen enjoyment
which he could scarcely have thought possible.
The perfect solitude, the fresh smell of the moist
earth, the soft patter of the rain in the swaying
trees, even the lash of the cold wet drops in
his face, seemed a truly fascinating change
after the sultry air of London in August, the
jaded faces of the people, the hurry and turmoil
of the dusty streets. A sense of physical and
mental oppression was removed, he felt at once
soothed and refreshed; the quick smooth

motion of the dog-cart had, in itself, a curiously
exhilarating influence; and he was, for the
time, carried away by the spell which Nature
exercises over more imaginative, finely-strung
temperaments.

But while his surroundings soothed and
charmed him on the one hand, on the other
he found them surprisingly and annoyingly
agitating. As he drove along, every field,
every tree, every turn of the road, every fresh
peep of the distant view, was the page of a
closed journal suddenly reopened before him—
for him to read with startling clearness all the
trifling events, all the thoughts, the dreams,
the little commonplace actions, the thousand
graphic, homely, pathetic details of daily life
in a now far-away past.

A dimly-remembered Self rose up before him,
and stood smiling in his face with a vividness
at once fascinating and unnerving; all his manhood and his manhood's experiences passed
away from him like a strange dream; the ten
years of his life out in India, the interesting,

bewildering knowledge of his fellow men and women acquired by dint of varied shocks and disillusions; the hopes, the pleasures, the thoughts—the outcome of these years, the Self of the Present—vanished with a swift, astonishing completeness. Far back into a bygone life his thoughts sped, and he was once more a boy driving home from the station after a day's shooting with his cousins at Cranthorpe; stowed away under the seat must be his gun— the gun for which he had so long pleaded, and of which he had been so short a time the proud possessor; near it must be reposing two or three rabbits which he was taking home to show in triumph to Judy in the cosy fire-lit schoolroom. He could picture her surprise and enthusiasm at his cleverness; how she would stand stroking the soft fur of the dear dead bunnies, looking with saddened serious face at their stiffening limbs and slowly glazing eyes, divided between deep distress at their harrowing fate, and alarm lest he should penetrate her feelings, and misconstrue them into

any lack of admiration for himself, or dis-
paragement of his actions. Ah, Judy—funny
little Judy!

A rift came in the clouds, and a pale watery
gleam struggled from behind it, lighting up
the country with a sudden shadowy brightness.
Higgins' face grew more cheerful, and Hugh
Lilcot, with an effort, roused himself and tried
to shake off his dreams. The rain was abating,
and, in the distance, a faint glimmer of sunshine quivered over the land, wreathing the
hills in purple mist and deepening the gold of
the corn. A little way off, dotted about here
and there, he could see the first offshoots of
the village—a few comfortable-looking, picturesque cottages standing well apart from one
another, each in the midst of its own garden
and embowered in its own little nest of fruit-
trees. In these houses, he remembered, the
better-class among the villagers used to reside,
considering it preferable to living further on,
in the midst of their poorer neighbours ; and
as the dog-cart turned the corner, and he

could see the scattered dwellings more clearly, he began trying to call to mind the inmates of some of the little homesteads at the time of his departure, their appearance, their particular characteristics, and their personal and peculiar cause for groaning under the dispensations of Providence.

But the deficiency of his memory on all these points, the impossibility, in many instances, of recalling even names which had at one time been daily upon his tongue, brought home to him completely the reality of the present, and the ghostly character of the dreamland in which he had been wandering; while, as the dog-cart sped on, and, having reached the village itself, clattered noisily up the principal street, he felt the shadowy nature of the past still more keenly. In that small world of which he had been such an important item, he was now a stranger among strangers. The few women who came to their cottage doors to stare at the cart as it went by, seemed all unknown to him; the men whom he passed on the road touched their hats

and strode on with stolid indifference, or stood
for a moment looking in idle curiosity after
this presumable visitor for the Hall. He tried
to remind himself that the telegram announcing
his arrival had only been sent that morning,
and the news, therefore, could not yet be
generally known; but this did not diminish the
fresh painfulness of the change which ten years
had been able to effect, and he felt in a measure
as a ghost may feel when it revisits the spot
on earth round which all its memories centre,
and sees what an easily effaced, pitifully insignificant mark the strivings, the dreams, the
pains of its life have left there. He experienced
an almost bitter yearning for one rough greet-
ing, one friendly glance, one smile of recognition
to pass over the faces of the people out of whose
lives he seemed to have gone so completely.
But all such satisfaction was denied him, and,
as the cart went on its way, the village was
soon left behind, without any sign of welcome
having been accorded to him by which he
might soothe his wounded vanity, or lessen the

sudden sense of isolation and loneliness which had crept over him.

Away, beyond the houses, the road wound abruptly up a hill; but instead of following its course further, the carriage turned to the left, and drew up before a high iron gate with quaint black lions surmounting the stone pillars on either side. This was speedily flung open from within by a neat, plump lodge-keeper, and the cart passed on under a dark avenue of fine old beeches.

Now, with every little gust of air, giant drops came pattering down from the branches above, and, poising his head so that they should roll off the brim of his hat without falling into his eyes, Hugh glanced eagerly and restlessly about him. Here, his critical gaze noted the trees were growing far too closely together; there, were several dead branches which should have been speedily lopped off and removed; the paths, he saw, had not been raked for some time and were green with weeds, while across them, in places, protruded boughs of overgrown

shrubs, producing a general effect of neglect
and disorder. All unconsciously he slipped
back into his boyish habit of thought. How
thoroughly the old place should be renovated
and improved when he himself became squire;
how different it would be with a business-like,
observant eye over it; how little chance there
should be in those days of its going to rack
and ruin through the carelessness of underlings:
—which reflections were followed by the same
boyish glow of shame at the thought that he
was calculating on a power which could only
come into his hands through the death of his
uncle, and this an uncle who had filled to him
the place of father. Hugh could appreciate
that, in adopting the orphan nephew who was
his heir, Sir Edward Lilcot must have first
overcome some personal feelings of bitterness
that his own child, being a girl, could not
inherit the property, and that thus to his
ceaseless kindness was due a still greater debt
of gratitude. Determining that his thoughts
should not again slip back into any of the

channels in which they had been wandering, Hugh turned to the groom at his side and suddenly launched into the only topic of conversation which occurred to him on the spur of the moment.

"Is this a horse which Miss Lilcot often drives?" he asked, nodding towards the animal which was now drawing him along at a speed which showed it had scented the proximity of its stables.

The groom looked reflectively at the horse's ears before he spoke.

"Well, no, sir," he answered, after a little consideration. "Miss Judy she has driven it, but she hasn't been in a dog-cart not this long while, and she has a pony for her basket-chaise."

"Her basket-chaise?" said Hugh, inquiringly. "That is something new. I don't remember anything of the sort when I went away. What has Miss Lilcot to ride just now?"

This time Higgins looked at him in unmistakable surprise.

" Miss Lilcot don't ever ride, sir," he said.

" Never ride ! " repeated Hugh, in his turn
unfeignedly astonished ; " never ride ! But
how long is it since she has given up riding ? "

" I can't say, sir," Higgins answered ; " but
Miss Lilcot hasn't been on a 'orse—oh, not this
long while."

Hugh relapsed into silence, revolving this
bit of information in secret dismay. Judy, who
never used to be happy off her saddle ; Judy,
whose one ambition was that when she grew
up she should be the best horsewoman in the
county ; Judy to have changed into a being who
never mounted a horse, who seemed even to
eschew anything so dashing as a dog-cart, who
chose in preference a quiet little basket-chaise,
drawn, doubtless by some sober, antediluvian
pony ! Ought he to have been prepared for
this astonishing change from her letters ? He
tried to call them to mind. Certainly, as far as
he could recollect now, she had not mentioned
having been out hunting, nor had she, of late
years, discussed horses with anything like her

former childish enthusiasm. He wondered this had not struck him before. But, then, she had written so little about herself and her own interests. Her correspondence consisted chiefly of scraps of news, and of questions concerning his own doings.

"Wonders will never cease!" commented Hugh, mentally. "I should have thought it impossible she could be so altered!" And over him, once more, crept that chilling sense of isolation which he had felt on being received as a stranger by his former friends in the village. Perhaps, after all, he had come back to the one place on earth he could view as home, only to find awaiting him at every turn a mere hollow mockery of all the old memories and associations he had clung to with an almost sacred love through all his years of absence. Even his uncle and Judy, he now reflected, must have changed with the rest of the world; and at least between the little maiden of fourteen he had left sobbing her heart out at his departure, and the decorous damsel of four-and-

twenty who must now be anticipating his
arrival in some excitement, there was probably
not any great connection. For the first time
he realized he was not about to be rapturously
received by the all-but father and sister he had
parted from so many years ago, but by an uncle
whose affection for him might reasonably have
lessened during that time, and by a strange
cousin with whom he had still to make
acquaintance.

And yet, on second thoughts, Hugh Lilcot
felt that this latter conclusion might be over-
hasty. Judy's letters to him had been essentially the letters of the Judy he remembered
merely grown older, and not those of a stranger
with whom he had nothing in common. He
had never till this moment thought of criticizing
the tone in which they were written; but now
a thousand little facts flashed across his memory
which inclined him to believe in the error of his
first decision. Those " home-letters " which he
had so treasured out in India were surely the
letters of a girl who looked upon him as a brother,

who remembered all his tastes, his pursuits, the
people he had cared for, the trifles which had
interested him. The Judy he had known could
not be entirely lost to him, though he must be
prepared to find her altered with the lapse of
time, and perhaps, just at first, to feel as though
he had never met her before——

"At any rate, in a few moments I shall
know the worst!" he assured himself with grim
resignation, as the dog-cart emerged from the
winding avenue, and he saw before him, on the
right, a green undulating sweep of park, with
the last remains of the shower drifting lightly
across it through the sunshine, and, on the
left, the rambling white building of Lilcot
Hall.

As the cart dashed up to the wide stone
porch, Hugh sprang to the ground. "You
can take my luggage round to the back!"
he called to the groom; and shaking off the
little streams of rain which were wandering
down his great travelling coat, he pushed open
the glass door and entered the house.

The stone hall in which he now found himself was low and somewhat dark; it was filled with the usual paraphernalia accumulated in the halls of country houses: along the walls were cases of stuffed birds, tiger-skins, antlers, prints, old weapons; and about on the chairs and tables were an untidy medley of hats, rugs, umbrellas, lawn-tennis racquets, balls, and shoes. On the further side of the hall were two white pillars; beyond them, across the passage, was a half-open door, through which a pale streak of sunshine was stealing out into the surrounding dimness.

Hugh shut the glass door behind him, and stood taking in every detail of the place. Nothing here seemed changed; it bore the self-same look it had borne on the morning, ten long years ago, when he had seen it last. The very fishing-tackle in the corner yonder looked as if it might be as he had left it; the big brown gloves lying on the table by his side were like his own, which he might have flung down as he went out. It seemed to him as though he had

been away but a few hours. A strange vague
fear of doing anything to break the spell of
this moment came over him. He waited there
motionless, hopelessly overcome by the unnerving feelings he had struggled to crush.
The place itself seemed spellbound. The stillness was unbroken. He could hear only the
drip, drip of the rain on the window-sill outside.

Suddenly, overpowered by an irresistible impulse, he stepped forward, raised his voice, and
called—as he would have called in those bygone
days—first softly, then more loudly, then impatiently—

"Judy! Judy! Judy!"

"For every link is lost between us twain
For ever, child, for ever!"

OWEN MEREDITH.

"There was one who looked
As if the earth had suddenly grown too large
For such a little humpbacked thing as she."

E. B. BROWNING.

CHAPTER II.

THE door across the passage opened quickly, the streak of sunshine widened; in the midst of it, for a moment, moved a dark figure; then the figure stepped away from the yellow haze and came swiftly forwards. Across the dark space of hall it approached noiselessly, then it passed out of the shadow, and the grey north light from the hall window fell sharply upon it.

Hugh Lilcot started. The spell had been broken by his own wilful act; in answer to his rash summons the presiding genius of the place had appeared, and for what species of creature he had thus invoked he felt superstitiously responsible.

Confronting him, he saw a grotesque little figure clad in black, the general sombreness of its appearance surmounted and relieved only by untidy masses of brown-gold hair. Big eyes were staring at him out of an old-young face; the creature's head seemed sunk into her chest; her arms were abnormally long. Standing there in the dim light, she looked some weird, uncanny imp of darkness which had suddenly risen up before him in mocking response to his cry.

Stifling an exclamation of surprise, Hugh Lilcot stared back at her in silence. Where could this strange apparition have sprung from? What was the possible explanation of her presence at Lilcot? Why did she come thus, like some evil omen, the first to greet him on the threshold of his old home? And why— he looked at her more earnestly—above all, why had he that painful, undefinable impression that her face was not unfamiliar to him?

Still doubting the evidence of his senses, he looked, till slowly, yet with a ghastly clearness,

there crept upon him the knowledge that this
strange and, to him, almost repulsive creature
had Judy's wild curly hair, grown a shade
darker; Judy's big, deep, beautiful eyes;—yes,
Judy's queer little dimple, about which he
used to torment her, appearing in the centre of
one thin, colourless cheek. In the shrunken,
wizened, deformed creature before him, he saw
a horrible, incredible travesty of the child who,
in her beauty and her gladness, had been to
him the dearest thing on earth.

He caught the handle of the door behind
him, and held it in a fierce, unconscious grasp.
Across his memory came pitilessly floating a
vision of the Judy of other days, tall, lithe,
graceful, a reckless tomboy with a face and
form which promised she would develop into an
unusually beautiful woman. Surely she was
standing before him again in her short frock, her
hair in fluffy disorder, her eyes alight with fun,
her face aglow with health and mischief. What
possible connection could there be between this
brilliant, childish creature and the unpleasant

piteous apparition he had seen a moment ago? Yet a great lump seemed to rise in his throat and choke him.

Then he became aware that, all this while, the girl was speaking to him—speaking to him with Judy's voice.

"Hugh," she was saying—"Hugh, is it really you? Oh, you have grown such a great broad creature I did not know you! I have been listening so anxiously for the cart, and I can't think how it was I never heard it drive up. I was waiting for you in the schoolroom —the old schoolroom. Hugh"—and a sudden piteousness came into the voice—"Hugh, don't you know me?"

Pulling himself together with a mighty effort, Hugh stepped forward and grasped the hand which he saw the girl was extending to him.

"Judy," he found himself saying with a voice which seemed to belong to some one else, "you can't think what it means to me to be home again. It feels almost too good to be true! I have looked forward to it for so long, and counted the days, the hours to it till—here I am at last! And it is so delightful seeing you again"—the voice to which he seemed listening trembled for a moment, and then reiterated its last sentence firmly—"so delightful to see you again, my little cousin!"

The girl cast upon him a **keen** quick glance, and the shrewd lines deepened about her compressed mouth. But Hugh, looking down at her, saw only round eyes smiling at him out of a child's soft face, pink dimpling cheeks like some delicate flower, red lips just parting for a merry laugh—till—slowly the bloom faded, the lips grew thin and sad, the cheeks were pale, drawn, old, and again the little wizened face was gazing at him through an unsteady mist of grey light.

Suddenly, **with an** undefinable change of manner, the girl had laid her hand on the sleeve of his coat.

"Why, you are dripping wet!" she exclaimed, in tones of exaggerated commiseration. "Take

off that damp thing at once, and come and dry
yourself by the fire."

She turned, and moved a few steps towards
the passage with an awkward limping gait, her
head and shoulders swaying in time to every
motion of her body, and the light from the
window revealing with cruel distinctness the
hump in the midst of her short crooked back.
Hugh looked away with a sickening sensation
of horror; mechanically he pulled off his coat
and hung it over a chair, then placed his hat on
a table near it. What was the explanation of
this nightmare? Like one dazed, he turned to
cross the hall, and discovered the small figure
had paused in the passage and was looking
back at him. Then a laugh rang in his ears
which had in it a ghostly echo of the merry
peal he had anticipated a moment ago.

"Hugh!" she exclaimed mockingly, "you
actually don't remember the way; you are
steering to the right! Why, your memory is
even more faulty than I was prepared for!" And
she pointed gaily towards the door opposite.

"Just imagine your having forgotten the way
to the old schoolroom! It really seems impossible, even after all these years. I suppose"
—she looked up in his face and laughed again
—"I shall discover many other things about
which your mind is now a blank ; but, of course,
to me this seems very extraordinary! Just at
present I feel as if you had been away for a
visit—rather a long one, certainly—but as if
you must remember all the little things which
happened before you left, and be dying to hear
all the bits of news which I have collected
while you were away. And I seem to have
such a lot to tell you, and such a lot I want
to hear! Now, one thing I am sure of—you
will not recognize the schoolroom in these
days."

She flung back the dark-panelled door, and
the red sunlight fell blindingly into Hugh's
face as he followed her into a large cheerful
room, with high French windows open to the
lawn and park. The stormy gleam rested upon
walls hung with pictures and china, upon pale

blue chairs, a yellow-draped piano, and wide silk curtains floating outspread in the breeze.

Hugh paused, and looked about him in bewilderment. No trace remained of the comfortable but severe-looking room he remembered. Where was the inky square table in the centre, over which Judy used to shed floods of rebellious tears, the dingy school-books in shelves along the walls, the stiff upright chairs, and, in a distant corner, the great globe whose recollection he even now hated? The whole aspect of the room was changed. The ink-stained, tear-washed table was replaced by little three-legged fragile successors with plush covers; the long book-shelves were hidden by dainty silk hangings; the chairs were of fantastic shapes and inviting appearance; and, in the spot formerly occupied by the objectionable globe, was a stand supporting a great cool palm, whose broad leaves swayed stiffly with the breeze which was filling the curtains. A profusion of delicious-smelling roses scented the air; the tables and piano were strewn with pho-

tographs, china animals, and the endless quaint
little knickknacks which women love; while the
gay chintzes, curtains, silk draperies, and flower-
bowls presented a curious medley of soft bright
colours, daringly but harmoniously blended.

Judy watched him closely as he glanced
round the room, and, reading a look of appreciation on his face, she clapped her hands with
almost childish delight.

" I knew you would be astonished!" she cried
excitedly. "This is my sitting-room now, and
I flatter myself it looks very different to what
it did in old days. There are no traces of
Fräulein Stutz left. I suppose, by the way,
you do remember Fräulein Stutz, your *ci-devant*
particular enemy and pet aversion? But I
don't believe years of foreign travel and blood-
curdling adventures can have quite effaced her
image from your breast! That is the very
chair she used to sit in, only you would never
know it now, all covered and cushioned; and
that sofa over yonder is the identical one on
which she used to stretch her elegant limbs

during Saturday afternoons, and which you once stuffed with onions in your zeal to add to her comfort. Don't you remember how furious she was? But, Hugh "—she paused abruptly — " come to the fire. I had it lighted on purpose for you. I thought you would feel the cold, coming from India; and, really, it is like winter to-day, after the grilling weather we have been having."

Drawing a chair towards her, she seated herself, and perched her feet on the edge of the fender. Hugh followed her advice, and, stepping upon the rug, meekly held out one damp sleeve to the feeble flame, while he pondered nervously with what remark he should break a silence on his part of which his cousin seemed blissfully unconscious, but of which he, himself, was painfully aware.

" Judy," he said at length, uttering the name with a somewhat halting attempt at glibness, " while you have been talking I have never had a chance of asking how Uncle Edward is. Do tell me now. Is he in?"

"Dad?" said Judy, looking up; "he has gone to a meeting of churchwardens. This year the other churchwardens are as fat as they very well can be; and I tell him it is important he should attend, as he is the sole representative of the lean kine! But he would have put it off if he had known earlier you were coming to-day; it was too late when your telegram arrived. He'll be back in an hour, I expect. But, Hugh"—and she suddenly jumped up from her chair—"I was forgetting: don't you want food of some sort? It is an hour-and-a-half past tea, and an hour-and-a-half to dinner. What kind of meal shall I offer you?"

Involuntarily Hugh smiled.

"I don't think I want anything. Unless, perhaps," he added doubtfully, "I have a glass of sherry. After swallowing all that damp, it might warm me up a bit; but I don't know—— "

Before he could finish his sentence, Judy was gone from the room.

A strange sense of relief came to Hugh. He breathed more freely. Seating himself in one of the low blue chairs, he gazed vaguely at the tall palm whose leaves knocked together with a faint grating noise. He still felt dazed.

Then he leant his forehead against his hand, and tried to collect his thoughts. Again he asked himself what was the explanation of this nightmare? Surely everything was unreal? He looked slowly about the room. In the daintiness and comfort of his surroundings there was an element of reality, but the incongruous little figure whose presence had so disturbed him must certainly be part of some disagreeable dream. If only she would not come back! He felt a sudden intolerable dread of hearing her returning footsteps.

Then, once more, he revolved the question to which his conversation with Higgins had first given rise. How far was he to blame in not having been more prepared for what had come upon him with overpowering suddenness? He tried to think calmly. He remembered

that, at the time of his departure for India,
there had been a good deal of fuss about Judy's
health. Ever since a fall she had had out hunting she had complained of pain in her back,
and had been made to lie down on the sofa
for an hour or two daily, which treatment she
had greatly resented, and against which he had
encouraged her rebellion. There had also, at
that date, he recollected, been a great discussion whether she should be allowed to go so
constantly for long rides. Symes, the country
doctor, had strongly advised her giving up
all horse exercise for a time at least; but Judy
had made such an indignant outcry against
this suggestion, and he, for his part, had
roundly denounced the doctor's folly in for-
bidding all healthy exertion, that Sir Edward,
always easily persuaded, had succumbed to
their joint reasoning. Later, in her letters to
India, Judy had groaned over the fact of
having been doomed to lie flat on her back for
a still longer time daily; and once, he remembered, she had given vent to an outburst

of angry intreaty. "I am sure it is the lying down which is *making* me ill," she had written in childish despair. " Do come home, Hugh, and defend me from this nonsense ! Fräulein and Symes talk dad over, and I have no one now to back me up. If only mother had lived, she would never have let me be bullied into an illness in this fashion." He could recall now how he had laughed over the letter, and over her graphic descriptions of the various methods by which she tried to evade " the pack of old woman's nonsense " to which she was being subjected, and how he had written back applauding her spirit in resisting it. To the pain of which she once or twice complained, he had attached but small importance. It was, he imagined, the ordinary weakness of a girl who was fast outgrowing her strength, and doubtless she was right in her belief that it was greatly due to the unhealthy life she was being forced to lead through the stupidity of the governess, for whom he still retained his boyish contempt.

Looking back now, he viewed the past in a different light; and as facts recurred in startling sequence to his mind, he could realize how the curvature of the spine, which had thus changed the bright, active child into a crippled, deformed woman, must have come on by slow degrees, and done its cruel work by such imperceptible stages, that it was scarcely strange no one should have thought of communicating its ultimate result to him as a new and startling fact; and that, moreover, while he had no suspicion of the truth, and had continued to put his own interpretation on remarks which might have enlightened him, his relations had never yet grasped the idea that he was not as well aware of what had taken place as were they themselves.

Judy alone, it struck him, might have had some misgivings on the subject. In one of her letters a short time before his return, she had certainly inquired whether he was prepared to find her grown up into a fright he would scarcely care to contemplate? but, from the facetious tone of the remark, he had looked upon it as a little conceited fun on the part of a girl happily conscious of her good looks, rather than as an observation to which any serious meaning could be attached. It was not likely, he assured himself, that he should ever have suspected the horrible reality. It was not possible that, unless the actual facts had been explained to him literally and mercilessly, he could ever have guessed what awaited him.

A slight sound in the room startled him. He looked up, to find Judy had returned, bearing a wine-glass and a decanter, which she proceeded to place on a chair by his side.

"There!" she announced, in a tone of triumph. "It was locked up, and dad had left the key in his coat upstairs. I had such a work to find it!"

She walked across to the chair she had before occupied, and once more seated herself with her feet perched upon the fender. Hugh, pouring out his glass of wine, was aware she

watched him intently. An unpleasant suspicion crossed his mind that she would discover
him to be preoccupied and ill at ease. He
plunged into a hurried attempt at conversation.

"I suppose you are a good bit alone, aren't
you?" he inquired irrelevantly.

A sudden look of amusement crept into Judy's
eyes.

"Oh, dear me, no!" she exclaimed emphatically. "I wish to goodness I were! It is still
our fate to have endless old relations planted on
us; and, you see, even in happier days I suffer
from the presence of a companion."

"Oh, that Miss Graham you have mentioned?" said Hugh, wondering if he were
talking naturally. "What is she like? A
modern substitute for the old Fräulein?"

Judy shrugged her high shoulders.

"As to that," she replied, "you will be
able to judge for yourself in a few days. My
Guardian Angel is away on a visit just now,
but I expect her back this week. I don't fancy

you ever met her, but she is a sort of cousin of yours and mine—Miss Nellie Graham."

Hugh tried to recollect if he had heard of any connections of that name.

"I'm sure you never met her," said Judy, divining his thoughts. "She is that trying climax of a trying species—a poor relation."

Hugh again sipped his sherry.

"It is well to know the worst. What ancient relatives are there here at present?"

"None!" Judy spoke with undisguised cheerfulness. "But there are two young ones whom I think you will be glad to meet. Dick Thornton has come over from Cranthorpe for a few days to see you, and Maud is here on a visit by herself."

"Maud?" said Hugh, thoughtfully, resting his glass against his knee. "I remember her engagement to Charlie Heathcote was announced just before I left home. I liked what I saw of Charlie; he seemed a good sort of chap. But I recollect Dick always seemed to consider his sister ought to have married

the other fellow. How strange it seems! I
suppose they have been jogging together in
the bonds of matrimony now for nine years.
How has the marriage turned out?"

"Oh, all right, I suppose," answered Judy,
carelessly. "They are supremely civil to each
other, which I imagine to be a public criterion
of domestic bliss. We see a good bit of Maud;
she often runs down here when Charlie is away
on circuit."

"That must be very jolly for you," responded
Hugh, and a pause ensued.

Judy hummed a tune, and tapped with her
foot on the bar of the fender, while Hugh
sought about anxiously in his brain for some
happy inspiration by which he might avoid the
threatened silence.

Although the quality of his conversation
might not be brilliant, there had been few
occasions in his life when he had found himself
actually at a loss for convenient small-talk;
but at the present moment, while there was
much that he wished to ask, and endless sub-

jects which might have readily suggested themselves to his mind, the odd, uncanny little
creature to whom his remarks must be ad-
dressed seemed to paralyze his ideas, and cause
him to feel curiously tongue-tied. Her flippant
manner, in contrast with her pathetic appearance, struck him as indescribably painful; and,
vainly as he tried to combat the knowledge, he
was more than ever aware she produced in him
a feeling of actual repulsion. This distressed
him. It was, in fact, no merely quiescent feeling, but a sense of something actively painful
and jarring—all the more so because the very
manliness in his nature rose in strong revolt
against any confession of its existence. A most
overpowering pity fought with a growing sense
of something akin to disgust with which her
movements inspired him; and she was, to all
appearance, so entirely at her ease, so un-
apologetic for her deficiencies, that he discovered it was difficult to conquer aversion by
compassion.

Men, in their likes and dislikes, are often—

as unconsciously as in their stronger passions—
swayed by some mere attribute of form which
has happened to appeal to or repel them. The
higher attributes with which, if the form
pleases them, they are willing to invest it, are
a mere afterthought. These, if real, may
strengthen and enchain their appreciation,
but seldom give birth to it; though, their
attention once stirred and arrested by this
material influence, they will be dominated for
good or evil by the mental qualities of the
being who has attracted them, and will then
fondly imagine it was those qualities which
swayed their inclination. All unknown to
Hugh, every one of his predilections and
antipathies were decided by some material
influence which he would often have found
it impossible to define. Though by nature
deliberate rather than impulsive, he was always
strongly biased; he had essentially no power
of analysis; he could not vivisect his friends
mentally or morally, and, having laid bare the
quaint mechanism of their inner being, pull it

coolly to pieces and decide which part of it was
satisfactory and understandable, and which was
the reverse; the world was, to him, split into
two clear divisions—the people he liked and
the people he disliked; the former he could
love with a generous, unswerving affection; the
latter he regarded with equally sweeping, unreasoning condemnation. But the cause that
had ruled under which of these two headings
his acquaintance should be classified was usually
remote and trivial, and the conclusions thus
arrived at curiously illogical; with women,
grace of motion and neatness of figure invariably led to his discovering them to be
possessed of exceptional spiritual excellence;
while irregularity of feature, awkward movements, or an ill-fitting bodice, had been sufficient
to reveal to him a whole category of moral
defects. It was true that ugliness of any sort
was at variance with his sense of harmony
and fitness; it was something disturbing and
irritating, a gross mistake—a crime on the
part of Nature which he had an innate belief

ought, by some means, to be eradicated from polite society, and any instance of which he was apt to exaggerate in proportion as the mere fact of its existence annoyed him.

This being so, had he returned to Lilcot to find his cousin grown up into much that his imagination had painted her, he would have been ready to believe her possessed of every quality he most appreciated in woman, and have given her, unquestioningly, an honest, staunch affection. Had he, on the other hand, returned to find her a normally plain girl, probably, after the first shock of disappointment, an influence from the love of former years would have reasserted itself, and aided him to discover some charm more subtle than the mere pink-and-whiteness of complexion and grace of limb which would have secured the approbation of his first glance. But the little creature who had suddenly obtruded her existence upon him, and whom he was studying now, as he sat abstractedly nursing his wine-glass, was to him an experience so new, so unpleasantly startling,

that he could not reconcile himself to it.   In
no wise could he connect her with the Judy of
his imagination; she failed to rouse in him any
sentiment of interest; she had no gentleness of
manner which appealed to his sympathy.   Had
it been fancy, he pondered, that the first time
when she spoke to him in the hall there had
been a shade of something pathetic in her face,
her voice?   Now she struck him as a childishly
happy creature, finding an almost silly satisfaction in trifles, talking in a light-hearted,
cynical manner which had in it even a flavour-
ing of conceit, and, after the momentary emotion
of their meeting was over, treating him as
though he were a schoolboy home for the
holidays.

He still continued to watch her moodily.
She was silent now, her arms folded across her
chest, her body bent slightly forwards.   A
thought came to him which filled him with a
certain surprise from its sheer novelty.   If only
this girl opposite to him had been attractive in
face and form, might not the remarks which

she had just been making to him, uttered in
the same tone, accompanied by the same
gestures, have appeared inexpressibly piquant
and charming? He found the idea curiously
disturbing. He knew that the impression she
had produced in his mind was not favourable,
and he was anxious to be just in his estimation
of her; but, after all, must not her physical
defects, which jarred upon him at every turn,
influence his judgment? Was it possible to
criticize her as impartially as if her deformity
did not first—little as he cared to own it—
produce in him feelings of irritation, and pre-
dispose him to misjudge her? For the first time
in his life he had approached some analysis of a
fellow-creature, and the process perplexed him.

He had heard it said that the peculiar
fascination of manner sometimes possessed by
people of unattractive appearance was an illus-
tration of how completely strong individuality
will assert itself over all physical disadvan-
tages. The body had been compared to an
instrument on which the soul plays its own

harmony. But was it difficult for an un-
imaginative mind to realize that possibly the
instrument, however faulty in structure, must
first be so constituted that it can lend itself
with ease to the interpretation of that inner
music, and that this may be as much a gift
of fortune, and as entirely beyond the power
of any excellence to ensure, as beauty itself?
What of those who have an instrument so
wholly out of tune with their needs that it can
never express the music of the soul which lies
silent within them—what medium have they
by which to touch the hearts of their fellows?
Must not theirs be a sorrow the greater because
it is seldom recognized as such?

In the midst of Hugh's reflections, Judy
glanced up unexpectedly, and surprised his
gaze fixed upon her. He looked hastily away,
but he had an uncomfortable belief that, in this
brief glance, she had read his present thoughts,
and was aware of the prejudice with which
he regarded her. Her next remark was not
calculated to reassure him.

"Hugh," she said, speaking in that sharp quick tone which always suggested a doubt respecting her seriousness, "I have been studying you, and—can you imagine it?—you are so altered I should never have known you! You looked such a boy when you went away, with such a chubby, innocent pink face, ánd a mythical moustache which nobody but yourself would believe in, and now you have come back an awe-inspiring veteran, with a skin like brown leather — excuse this inventory — a ferocious moustache, at least an inch too long for true beauty, a fierce military expression, and I swear if I looked closer I could discover carefully concealed grey hairs resting on your venerable head! It is most strange, and I cannot quite get used to you! However, you may be equally surprised at the way I have developed in these years. Tell me "—she looked him full in the face—" do you find me much altered?"

Was there a spice of malice in her tone, or did she ask the question in all the innocence of a mind incredibly free from self-consciousness? It was a point which Hugh found impossible to decide; but he felt, not unreasonably, annoyed with her for putting him in such an awkward position. Thinking of her remark in the letter he had received just before his return, he hurriedly made up his mind it would not be wise to openly evade the truth.

"Yes," he said, after a pause, "I naturally do find you changed, and I am sorry—very sorry."

She could take that as an intentionally sympathetic remark, or as a mere pointless little speech—whichever she liked, he reflected.

Judy reached out her hand, and lifting one of the roses out of a glass bowl by her side, rolled its green stem round and round between her finger and thumb.

"You mean," she said slowly, watching the flower which was helplessly shedding its petals, "that you were utterly unprepared to find"—she stopped, and then, giving an awkward laugh, pointed with the rose over her shoulder in the direction of her crooked back—"to find

Punch instead of Judy? Eh? Yes," she went
on quickly, " I believe I am not exactly beautiful ; but, as I cannot see myself, it is those who
can see me who are to be pitied! I forgot
I ought to apologize to you! Down here every
one is so used to me, they are contented to
take me as I am. Of course, in society I
might be a regular dot-and-go-one; but I don't
trouble society, and I find what one has never
tasted one has never acquired a taste for!
Don't you admire the simplicity of my choice ?
Arcadia, without even the shepherds and
shepherdesses ! "

She flung the rose into the centre of the fire,
and watched, with a look of half-spiteful enjoyment on her face, while it lay quivering
like a thing in torture, till, with a sudden burst
of flame, it shrivelled up and disappeared.

Hugh hesitated with regard to his next
remark. He was greatly surprised that she
should have openly referred to her deformity,
and still more astounded that she could discuss
it in her usual off-hand, light-hearted tone.

Yet, since she had deliberately done this, might not he hazard a straightforward question which he was now desirous to ask ?

" Do you suffer at all ? " he inquired at length.

A slight frown passed over Judy's face. Then she rose up from her chair and stretched herself leisurely before she spoke.

" Suffer ? " she replied evasively. " Isn't pain a mere question of what one is or is not used to ? " She moved slowly away towards the window. " Do you know that the shower is over ? Come and see how lovely the old place looks ! There will be a glorious sunset to-night ; the clouds are so grand and stormy."

Hugh, rising, followed her, and stepped outside on to the wet terrace. The rain had entirely ceased. On the lawn the flower-beds lay disordered, their freshness and beauty gone from them ; the roses up the great basket-bed in the centre hanging their shamed heads, the jasmine sprays swinging idly beneath their weight of silver drops. Beyond the wire fence

at the foot of the lawn lay the park, green and
moist in a veil of hazy sunshine, the lake cutting
it sharply in sunder with wide still waters—
first tinted palely by wavering pink reflections
from the clouds overhead, then flashing into
momentary fire as they rushed over a foaming
weir, next lying grey and cold in the river
which bore them away. Further, lay the
village, dim like a phantom city, its houses
shrouded in saffron mist, the spire of the
church like a tongue of blue flame in its midst.
All around reigned a great stillness. From
the weir came a murmur of tumbling waters ;
nearer, a wood-pigeon cooed in complaining
tones.

Why, as Hugh stood drinking in the beauty
of the scene before him, did there come ringing
in his ears, in such a strange unreasoning
manner, a verse of the time-honoured missionary
hymn which he had often sung, with all the
strength of a clear boyish treble, and all the
fervour of a fresh boyish heart, down in the old
church yonder, in bygone days ?—

> " What though the spicy breezes
>   Blow soft o'er Ceylon's isle,
>   Though every prospect pleases,
>   And only man is vile ! "

" And only man is vile—and only man is vile ! "—why should that line keep repeating itself with such meaningless, absurd persistency ?

Suddenly he saw the sequence of ideas. From the smiling sunlit park he glanced to the distorted little human figure beside him. Judy stood with her head thrown back, her gaze fixed on a black jagged cloud which was hurrying across the washed-out blue-grey heavens. A loose lock of hair waved to and fro on her forehead ; her lips were apart ; on her face was a rapt, eager expression which made her look older, more grotesque, more uncanny than ever. The still beauty of the summer's evening may have stirred in her some vein of sentiment ; yearnings and fancies may have been floating through her brain, which, had her form been fairer, would have lent an exquisite glow to her cheeks, a lovelier light to her eyes ; but, dreaming thus in the mellow evening light, with that far-away smile on her upturned face, she seemed to Hugh only comically, pitiably ridiculous.

He turned again to the restful landscape. Certainly the human element alone marred an otherwise perfect scene. It was cruelly pathetic that, in this dreamy, beautiful bit of the world should have grown up a living embodiment of bitterest human affliction and failure—the failure of a glad young life. A new-born pity came to him for this girl who did not pity herself, for this blighted existence which knew so little of the *joy of being*, now—and for ever —lost to it. All other feelings vanished before an unutterable compassion. The very peacefulness of the scene before him suddenly hurt him with its placid, imperturbable calm. In the presence of a great human sorrow Nature is so pitiless, so cold; she stabs us with her smiling superiority.

Hugh moved nearer to the girl, who seemed lost in the enjoyment of the scene before her, and broke ruthlessly upon her silence.

"Judy," he remarked abruptly, "I want to tell you one thing—I want you always to know and feel one thing—that all these years I have been away have made no difference between us as far as I am concerned; all the friends I have made, all that has happened to me during that time while you have been leading a quiet uneventful life here in the old home, have not changed my former affections or really altered me. My appearance may be different, but my heart is much the same as in old days! I do want you to feel that. We must be just the same brother and sister we were then—more so, perhaps, because at that time, while you were a child, I was, or thought myself, a man; now no such gulf separates us, we shall be far better able to understand and get on with each other."

Then, having in the kindness of his heart uttered this lie, and half persuaded himself that he believed it, he slipped his arm about the motionless little figure beside him, and drawing her closer to him, kissed her once—twice.

" Two lovers, soon after their happy union, are separated by death. How vivid is the faith of the survivor that they shall meet again ! Surely somewhere they shall be reunited. Is there not space enough—are there not stars enough in the wide heavens? And all they want is a little space to love in—some foothold given them in creation. All the rest of their eternal joy they carry with them—such joy as it would surely be amazing waste and prodigality to let fall out of the universe.

" What if they had lived and loved a little longer on the earth ? Perhaps the star would not have been wanted."
—THORNDALE.

CHAPTER III.

MAUD HEATHCOTE sat in a low chair with her head nestled against a large soft cushion. There was no fire in the grate opposite which she was seated—the position was one she had adopted out of sheer force of habit—yet she was studying the black bars before her as intently as though beyond them lay those fire-pictures we all love to trace in the crimson coal; pictures faulty in anatomy as they are gorgeous in colouring, and which can adapt themselves so strangely to illustrate our passing fancies.

Behind her, over the dressing-table, one tiny jet of gas burnt dimly, the window-curtains were drawn back, and, outside, the night lay, oppressive in its blackness, its intense silence.

From time to time she turned to glance back
at it restlessly, as though she found some unpleasant fascination in its impenetrable gloom.
Then she leant her head once more wearily
against the large cushion. Her white dressing-
gown fell about her in loose folds; its trans-
parent lace lay lightly upon her full throat
and arms.

There is a weariness of body which steeps
the brain in a languor in itself soothing, which
brings with it a foreshadowing of the forgetful-
ness of sleep, so that we no longer see life in
its grim nakedness, no longer fret so fiercely
over its aches and pains. If Maud Heathcote,
at the close of her thirty-five summers, had
learnt to appreciate the callousness which comes
through bodily fatigue, to-night, in the solitude
of her room, she seemed courting its influence
in vain. The gaslight which shone dimly on
her dark, handsome head, and fell more palely
still on the folds of her white gown, revealed
also upon her face a look which told that the
brain within was too active, that physical

weariness had not yet lulled it into a state of desirable calm.

There came a low tap at the door; it opened, and Judy, a small figure in pink and grey, appeared on the threshold. She held a candle, which she paused to place on the chest of drawers and extinguish. Her tea-gown hanging loosely from her shoulders partially hid her deformity. She looked like a child. But, as she stepped forwards, the grey train swept after her with a spasmodic movement, and, with each step, the cords hanging from her waist swung sharply from side to side.

She nodded towards the open window.

" Why this inclination for airiness ? " she inquired.

Maud looked at her visitor with a smile.

" Perhaps the weather has changed again," she answered absently ; " but I felt oppressed, so I opened both windows, as you see. How long you have been coming up, Judy ! "

" I was talking to dad," Judy answered, settling her small person on the soft fur rug.

No sooner had she done so, however, than she rose again, reached a match-box off the mantelpiece, and knelt down before the black grate.

"What are you doing?" Maud asked, laying a detaining hand on her arm. "It is warm to-night."

"Why are you shivering?" demanded Judy; and soon a small bright flame was curling stealthily up through the sticks and coal, and a few preparatory crackles and pops in its wake gave warning of louder ones to follow.

Then Judy rose, walked to the window nearest to the fireplace, closed it, drew the curtains, and came back to resume her former position on the rug.

"Now I come to think of it," said Maud, "I believe I have grown cold, but I did not know it till you spoke. I thought it warm when I came from downstairs! Perhaps I am tired."

Judy leant forward and poked two sticks further into the fire.

" What were you thinking about when I came in ?" she asked.

" What was I thinking about ?" repeated Maud. " A comprehensive question! Oh, many things, my dear! Things belonging to the past and present. At the precise moment you opened the door, I believe I was considering Hugh amongst others."

" What of him ?"

Maud opened a Japanese fan which lay upon her lap, and looked at its flaming red-and-yellow design.

" Hugh has always reminded me," she answered, " of the saying that the world accepts us at the price we put upon ourselves. He is so essentially a being who has labelled himself a valuable acquisition to the human race, and who takes an inoffensive pleasure in our acceptance of his valuation. If you wish for further criticism, I should say he is good-looking, good-hearted, a decided gentleman. I think "—a look of amusement came into her face—" he would imagine himself far-seeing

when he is most prejudiced; determined
when he is hopelessly obstinate; shrewd when
he takes rapid, unreasoning impressions. In
short, he is much what, a few years back, I
should have imagined he would grow up into."

Judy did not answer immediately.

"He is altered," she said at length; "I
cannot feel him the same. For one thing"—
she made a slight grimace—"he dislikes me."

Maud turned a quick, surprised glance
towards her.

"Sheer imagination!" she pronounced.

"He dislikes me," persisted Judy, obstinately.
"My dear Maud, our respected cousin is a poor
hand at concealing his feelings! I was a truly
terrible shock to him. Poor boy! It was
rather unfair he was not warned what to expect!" She gave a little shrill laugh. "Dad
was very talkative this evening after you came
up. I heard him explaining to Hugh that I
was very delicate, and that my spine was inclined to be troublesome—it would require care
to set it right—after which he aired his favourite

hobby that I am the living image of that old portrait of Margaret Lilcot hanging outside my room in the north wing. He asked Hugh if the likeness were not remarkable? Poor Hugh! all his suaveness deserted him. I had to come to the rescue."

"What did you say?"

"I? I crossed the room and informed him that he must see the resemblance, as I had often been mistaken for the original of the picture! His face was a study!"

Maud's hand left the fan with which it had been playing, and rested on Judy's head with a light caressing touch.

"Hugh must have made a great many friends we know nothing about, and seen a lot of the world while he was away. He will find us very humdrum here, and be very bored after the first week," said Judy.

Receiving no answer, she looked up inquiringly into Maud's face.

"What else were you thinking about when I arrived? You are depressed to-night."

Maud roused herself with an obvious effort.

" I am, and I have been spending the last hour trying to discover the exact cause of my depression, without arriving at any conclusion whatsoever." She opened and shut the fan upon her lap with a faint crisp noise. " To-night Hugh seemed to bring back a whiff of the past. I cannot resist sentimentalizing over bygone days, and wishing I were a girl again, though probably I was not one degree happier then than I am now. But one's nature is so incomprehensible! I do not believe I am by any means a discontented, morbid creature, yet, directly I allow myself to think, I find I am hungering, aching for happiness with a terrible sense of some want in my life which has never yet been satisfied. I imagine this is chronic to most human beings"—she began fanning herself swiftly. " When I was a girl I used to believe it must be the natural craving in woman's nature for love; that, when I had felt some great all-absorbing devotion for another human being, everything would be

different. I fancied that was the real secret
of life—at least to a woman. And when "—her
eyes saddened—" there came to me, too, a knowledge of all the inexplicable happiness love can
give, I thought I had truly found the clue to
life's previous emptiness. On a sudden it had
grown so grand, so complete, so intoxicating,
its perfection more than satisfied me. And yet,
after all, there came a day when, without
warning, the old hunger awoke within me,
awoke with a new savage strength such as it
had never possessed before, and which simply
appalled me. I knew then that it had been
lulled, drugged into quiescence for a time, but
that all my fancied content had been a mere
passing sensation. The awakening was not
pleasant." She paused. " I think work is the
only drug we could take in comfortable repeated
quantities, so that it could dull that odd pang
of hunger for any length of time. Love is a
truly wonderful anæsthetic, but it is too power-
ful, too bewildering; its effects wear off too
soon."

Judy studied her face with a curious little smile.

"I wonder," she observed, "how this medicinal conversation would strike Hugh. He was questioning me about your marriage— if it had turned out a success? I answered in the affirmative, which was a satisfaction to him, as he approved of Charlie."

Maud laughed.

"Approved of Charlie!" she said. "Who wouldn't? who could do otherwise than 'approve of Charlie'? The very idea is, in itself, absurd! Charlie strikes me as all the most exacting on-looker could wish. We have been a most exemplary couple. In public we appear side by side, in private we neither nag nor worry each other; after nine years of marriage we are capital friends; what more can anybody desire or expect? And yet "— her tone grew more animated—" and yet I am for ever looking round me in the world at the other amiable, smiling, exemplary married couples—people whose very aspect seems a sort of perpetual

advertisement of the success of matrimony—
and wonder, and *die* to know if the experience
of their secret souls has been as perplexing as
that which mine has undergone. Judy! it is
said that each soul comes into being—grows
sentient—develops—matures—to pass through
the furnace of Passion and issue thence brute
or divine. In woman this crucial test—love—
has been called 'an aspiration after the Beautiful,' a 'Religion,' a 'Prayer;' in man it has
been adequately symbolized in terms scarcely
so flattering and certainly less poetic! But,
whatever one's condition during the process,
what of the many souls who come forth from
it far from either brute or divine—transformed
into some strange mongrel breed, impossible to
classify? What of them?

"To-night"—she spoke more quickly, as
though retailing some previous train of thought
—"to-night let me amuse myself, Judy, by reading my heart aloud. Looking back at my life-
story, it has, I suppose, been a very ordinary
one. I was, as you know, engaged to Hubert

Cox. I met him in my first season, when I
went up to London. He was a great friend
of Dick's. I saw him constantly; he became
devoted to me; I was surprised and flattered.
From having been snubbed by my brothers
and ordered about by my governess, I found
myself exalted into the position of a small
queen—a deity, rather—while the happiness of
a man, in every sense my superior, depended
on the tone of my voice, on the turn of my
head, upon a smile, a glance bestowed at the
moment he craved it. I felt a strange tenderness towards this being who could idealize me
so foolishly, a certain compassionate gratitude;
I grew to love him with what seems to me now
an impertinent patronizing affection—a girl's
love, in short, a mere appreciation of being
appreciated.

" Afterwards came the woman's love.

" When I grew to know Charlie Heathcote,
I learnt that hitherto I had been loved; now
I, in my turn, must love. Therein lies a vast
difference. I could not marry Hubert after

that knowledge came to me. I have often
thought that Nature's greatest cruelty to woman
lies in the fact that, the purer one's life, of very
necessity the more keenly does one suffer when
love comes, the more imperative it is to be true
to the dictates of that love. At that time I
did not believe that Charlie loved me, but
I realized all that was highest in my nature
demanded I should abide by what I felt for
him. I think "—she turned slowly, a reflection
from the silk cushion on which her head rested
shed a faint glow over her cheek—" the sorrow
of unrequited affection is to me the most
mysterious, most sacred of all sorrows. It is
a strangely refining influence in life—at once
so humiliating in its folly, so grand in its self-
oblivion! In all my wretchedness—and that
bit of my life was very wretched—I knew that
I was glad to have lived, if only to have known
this strange pain. It is curious trying to recall
that state of feeling—that wonderful moment
in life when Self becomes extinguished in some
great affection! It is as though one had sprung

from an insignificant creature, half awake, half
alive, into some nobler being; a being one
cannot understand, but must needs reverence.
Afterwards, when my love grew happier, it
was a shade less fine, but not one whit less
wonderful! Oh, the unselfish egotism of love
is so marvellous—the way we cease to feel for
ourselves and become savagely egotistical for
the being in whom our individuality has become
merged! Yet," and her voice took a gentler
tone, " as it is the only time in our lives when
Self genuinely ceases to exist, when we breathe
and see and feel and know only for another,
when we touch happiness or touch suffering
only through the medium of another, so it is
the most beautiful, the most exquisite time of
life, whether in its pain or in its joy!"

She paused, as though exhausted with the
vehemence with which she had spoken, then
continued more slowly, and with a smile upon
her lips.

" And now," she said, "now, as I tell you,
we are capital friends—capital. I sit opposite

Charlie and think what a success our marriage
has been; how satisfactorily—being both of us
even-tempered, sensible, respectably-constituted
people—we have managed to steer clear of all
the little currents and whirlpools in which our
less praiseworthy neighbours have come to grief,
publicly or privately. And I sit opposite to him
too, and wonder, with a great ever-growing
astonishment, whether it was for that little
being over there — spectacles, smoking-coat,
slippers complete—that I once knew all those
sublime feelings, all those poetical thoughts, all
that ideal devotion; whether, by some extraordinary freak of nature, he was the instrument
which developed my soul within me! Don't
misunderstand me—I am really fond of Charlie;
he has been, and is, my best friend, and I am
grateful to him for all his goodness to me; I
think I would go through misery sooner than
he should suffer any pain from which I could
save him; but that does not lessen the marvel
of it—for that little harmless, amiable, ordinary
nonentity I suffered all that feverish pain, I

felt all that passionate devotion, I knew all that
divine, incomprehensible unselfishness — for
that—that ! "

Again she paused.

" Do married people usually feel this when
they dare to think ?   Does he feel it about me,
I wonder ? "

Judy bent towards the fire, and held out a
thin little hand to the blaze.

" The mistake in your life," she remarked
sapiently, " seems to have been that you did
not marry Hubert Cox."

" But, my dear child," exclaimed Maud, " I
was not in love with him !   You talk as though
one could coolly and rationally decide who one
is to love.   As well accuse me of not having
chosen my own mother wisely !   I liked
Hubert ; I loved Charlie.   Fate so arranged
matters — that is all I know ; and I imagine
Fate arranged them well.   Consult the world's
verdict ; my marriage with Charlie has answered admirably ; my marriage with Hubert,
I feel, might have been a *fiasco.*   When two

people, each possessing strong individuality, endeavour to become one, the result is, of necessity, a failure. The very fact that their natures cannot be fashioned on the same pattern, and that, being strong, they must pull all the more powerfully in different directions, brings this to pass. In a truly happy marriage there is always—clearly defined—the leader and the led."

" Maud," said Judy, " if you had had a child, you would have felt differently."

Maud shook her head impatiently.

" Judy," she said, " for the first time you think you have discovered I am hard, embittered, disappointed. To-night you judge me critically because, for once, I have spoken my exact thoughts—an unwise act we are seldom guilty of! We women become shams even to our own selves; we do not venture to whisper to our own hearts what they themselves feel. The key-note of our lives is so often, ' Never think; frivol, work, suffer, do what you please, only shun thought. Thought drags Truth so pointedly under one's ken, and Truth is often objectionable—indecent!'

"No," she continued more seriously, "I am truly fond of Charlie. I see clearly there are few lives which have run side by side more harmoniously than ours; yet, can you not grasp the idea that affection is one thing, love another? Love, of its very nature, is both too splendid, too absurd, for everyday life. Above everything in this world, we must be rational! We cannot live perpetually in a state of ecstatics! Love, they say, is heaven or hell (more correctly, contains a whiff of both places); as we are now constituted, we could not breathe long in either the rarefied atmosphere of the former, or the fiery torment of the latter; having tried both, with a start of surprise we find ourselves back again, vaguely stunned, greatly bewildered, generally relieved, in this quiet commonplace old earth of ours. That is all!"

She rose up, and stood leaning against the mantelpiece. Her gown fell about her tall figure in straight folds. The firelight played softly upon her face.

" No, Judy, I did not want a child to make me happier. Of all the outrageously egotistical ideas that human beings become possessed with, the most outrageous seems to me that we wish to create a life solely because it may make our own happier or richer in interest. Mark you, one never hears a lament over the absence of children on the score that, life being a priceless blessing, it is sad that any chance of legally and advantageously bestowing this inestimable boon should be wasted—*that* is never the cause of regret; it is that children form such a link between husband and wife, that children call out the best side of woman's nature, that children form such an interest, such an occupation ! As if, possibly, we women might not love our husbands sufficiently for their own sakes ; as if there were not already enough people in this over-populated world whereon to vent our latent sympathy and tenderness ; as if we could not find enough work without wishing to create more lives merely to give us something to do! There are times "—she leant her face against her arm—" when I have longed, with that longing which only comes to a woman after marriage, to know the warm clinging love of a little child who was my own—my own, a bit of my own flesh, a bit of my own soul, my life given back to me again, fresh and unsullied, to train up into something nobler, purer than the old life now can ever be. But I recognize that those feelings, though natural, were solely egotistical. It was for my own selfish happiness I felt that wish, with my unimpassioned reason I am glad not to be the originator of a race of beings to strive—suffer——— "

From the rug where she sat, Judy looked up at the tall figure above her. Her glance travelled slowly from the dark, well-poised head to the shapely, bronze-shod feet resting in the fur beside her.

" Then," she said, " you, who to all appearance, and according to your own showing, have had, as lives go, a smooth, easy, successful existence, you look upon life as a curse, not a blessing; you consider that each smiling face conceals a tragedy, the only difference being that some are dramatic, poetical tragedies, others prosaic, uninteresting ones—like yours, like mine?"

For a moment Maud was silent. When at length she spoke, her voice had grown very soft.

"Until we understand life, how shall we dare to judge life?—we, who are so utterly in the dark about everything, that when we come to any of the great problems of existence, there is no one subject on which we ever say, save through ignorance, '*I know*.' I was merely stating my own feelings, not wishing to make over-bold assertions. Life, as I see it at present, seems interesting, not happy, except in clear brief patches; and there is something to me so piteous, so very piteous, in the way young things pant and fight for happiness. They cannot—they will not believe life to be other-

wise than the brilliant treasure their heart
paints it; yet they feel so keenly the dis-
crepancy between what it is and what they
fancy it should be, that each in his turn
imagines he alone is unfortunate, he alone
is plagued above his fellows. As we grow
older we have at least learnt that to none of
us is existence a bed of roses; that "—her eyes
seemed to rest unconsciously on Judy—" in the
world around us those who laugh most are not
the happiest, but the bravest."

Again there was silence in the room. Judy
bent forward to pick up a charred stick which
had fallen into the fender, and dropped it back
amongst the bright flames.

"Maud," she said at length, looking up with
a slightly supercilious smile, " I want to know,
don't you find people irritating when—to dis-
course in clerical language—they talk away to
you about ' resignation under our manifold
afflictions, and gratitude to Providence for the
many blessings we enjoy'? How I know by
heart all the illogical twaddle which our elderly

relations accumulate for my benefit, and which, when it fails to amuse, irritates me beyond measure! How I have longed to ask them what they mean! I understand what has to be borne may as well be borne with unpretentious pluck, but why pretend to be flattered at being afflicted? and why be so overwhelmingly grateful when we are allowed a little peace and rest?." She spoke with quick angry emphasis. "As to gratitude to Providence for every little scrap of happiness or good luck which may be ours—there is quite a little hobby on the subject running through all classes! The clergy are never quite so eloquent on any other matter; with canting villagers it is the favourite topic; in our own set, though not so much talked about, it is, on account of our superior advantages, all the more recognized as a state of mind particularly incumbent upon us to cultivate. And why? To me, gratitude for our so-called blessings seems simply gratitude for not being tormented, thankfulness for exemption from some of the evils with which our fellow-creatures are being cruelly plagued! I feel I have a right to be happy; that, having had this existence thrust upon me willy-nilly, I have a right to demand and expect that it should be a pleasant one, or to be indignant at the unkind treatment I have received. When I am happy, I consider I am receiving my right, my due; when I am miserable, I am overpowered by a sense of injury and ill-usage —I feel defiant, rebellious.

"I was thinking," she added a moment afterwards, "when Mrs. Hutchins in the village, who has lost the use of her limbs from rheumatism, cants away to me about having so much cause to be thankful because she is not also blind like her neighbour Mrs. Dyke, I always find myself puzzling over her point of view. If I were Mrs. Hutchins I should not be grateful for not having been plagued more, but indignant at having been plagued at all."

She twisted the cord of her tea-gown round her wrist, then unwound it, and looked absently at the mark it had left.

"When people are determined to see one point of view, and one only," she went on, "it is marvellous how much they will overlook in the attempt. The other day a Methodist preacher who is staying at the blacksmith's presented me with a tract. In it was a story of the pious Dr. Paley, who, seeing some shrimps on the seashore at Allonby looking exceedingly lively, stood gazing at them, and expatiating on the goodness of Providence, 'who could make even shrimps so happy.' Granting that the rather unwarrantable assumption of the good gentleman was correct, and that unusual activity in shrimps is a sign of boundless bliss, why—by all that is rational!—was he obstinately to shut his eyes to the anomaly, that if Providence was to be praised for making a shrimp lively, could Providence be entirely exonerated for allowing neighbouring starfish which had been cast ashore to lie in torture in the hot sun? The good unthinking world is to me so like that little tract in the way it skirts round all small facts which are at variance with its pet theories, and ignores their existence so gracefully—so very gracefully!"

Maud's gaze turned from the fire and rested again somewhat sadly upon Judy.

"Ah, well," she said, "though to-night I have indulged myself by a refreshing grumble about the general queerness of life, let me tell you, none the less, how I view it. It reminds me of a plant struggling up through the dark mould to the Light, not knowing what the Light may be, not able to tell after what it is striving, but struggling on instinctively, blindly, trustfully—up—up to something higher and better than it can ever dream. Thus, though life may be something in which we think we should never have embarked of our own free will, yet, finding ourselves launched in it, we feel it is well worth going through with bravely and trustfully. Within each of us lies a germ of the May-be—a divine essence which we may develop into something beautiful and strong, or ruthlessly crush and kill. If sorrow and

suffering help to develop this divine essence
more quickly and perfectly, then welcome
sorrow and suffering ! "

The firelight quivered in her eyes. They
had grown like moist amber.

"If we would only recognize it," she continued, still looking dreamily at Judy, "the
course which leads up to the Light is so
different for every one of us. We have each
our own ideal to follow; to each of us the
method of developing what is divine within
us is entirely different from that which our
neighbour should adopt. When we once
thoroughly realize this, we cease ever to
criticize our neighbours' actions or to comfort-
ably mould our own by theirs; for, no matter
what our creed, no matter what our belief or
absence of belief, we have each some distinct
law of our inner consciousness to follow ; until
we have wilfully blunted our perceptions, we
can always know clearly whether we are
strengthening or weakening what is noblest
in us. And the real battle of life consists in

these trivial struggles to be true to what is
highest in us, for by them we build up our
characters, till, when a great trial comes, we
test the worth or the worthlessness of what we
have been gradually constructing." She folded
up the fan and laid it back upon the mantelpiece. "And oh," she said, "the difficulty
of being true to that law of our own hearts!
An infinitesimal swerving from our secret code
of honour, a little convenient leaning to our
neighbour's views, a slight, all but unconscious
acting of what we wish to seem, and we are so
often more sincere, more honourable in the eyes
of our fellow-creatures, than when we adhere
with tears and torture to that private course
of right."

Judy rose up slowly and walked across to
the open window. She pushed it further up
and looked out at the night. A breeze was
stirring the trees near at hand; they were
swaying and whispering in the darkness. The
soft patter of raindrops was audible on the
laurel bushes down below.

She drew herself up on to the window-sill and leant far out, till the fresh damp air blew in her face, and the drops rebounding off a neighbouring pipe fell with a cold splash upon her forehead. Then, with her body still outside, she looked away from the great pall of darkness which was enveloping that outer world, back into the room where the firelight was bathing Maud's white figure in a rosy glow.

"Well," she remarked, "we have discussed weighty matters to-night—Life and Love! Life, we conclude, remains a mystery. Love" —she looked back at the night—"we discover to be a folly from which every sane woman should pray to be defended!"

Maud pushed her armchair aside and stepped away from the fire.

"But," she said, "it is a beautiful folly!"

She moved slowly towards the window; then, as she discovered the position in which Judy had perched herself, her step quickened.

"My dear child!" she exclaimed, "even if life is not altogether satisfactory, I cannot

guarantee any advantage you will ensure by
breaking your neck to-night!"

Judy slid leisurely back into the room, but
without the vestige of a smile upon her serious
little face, and for a short breathing space the
two women stood silently listening to the
ghostly whisperings of breeze and rain which
stole through the darkness. Confronting each
other thus, they afforded a strange contrast.
Maud, with the firelight behind her, white,
statuesque, massive; Judy, a shrunken grey
figure, framed by the dark night.

Then Maud leant down and kissed her.

"You look tired," she said remorsefully, "and
I have been keeping you up!"

Judy shook her head. "I'm not tired!"
she contradicted emphatically; then, stepping
back, she shut the window behind her and
drew the curtains across it; next she proceeded
to turn up the gas and poke up the fire, after
which, giving one glance round to assure
herself everything looked comfortable, she lit
her candle and limped from the room.

A few moments later, Hugh, in his smoking-coat and a yellow-back under his arm, crept up the staircase leading from the hall. The lights had been put out, and the house was in darkness. He trod cautiously, partly from an anxiety not to extinguish the flame of his newly-lighted candle, and partly from a desire not to wake the slumbering inmates of the house by over-much creaking of the oak steps beneath his tread. The staircase up which he was making his way, wound past the north wing, where it branched into two narrower flights, leading in one direction to the servants' rooms over-looking the stables, and, in another, to a part of the house known as the Tower, where he was established in his old quarters. As he turned the corner approaching the landing, an incautiously quick movement of which he was guilty extinguished the sickly flame on which he depended, and, with a smothered exclamation of annoyance, he prepared to descend once more to the hall in search of the matches he remembered having left there. At the same moment, however, he became aware he was not in total darkness; a faint light glimmered from the landing above and shone dimly on the steps where he stood. Hoping to discover some servant within call who could save him from a search in the dark downstairs, he again turned, and, running up a few steps, peered anxiously in the direction whence the light came.

Halfway down the dim passage before him stood Judy. Her quaint grey gown clung about her misshapen figure, her wide hanging sleeves were outspread like wings. She held a candle at arm's length above her head, and the flame flickered while she stared up at a large portrait which hung on the wall in front of her.

From the position in which he stood, Hugh could see the portrait plainly. It was one he remembered well, and one which had been, that very evening, recalled more strongly to his memory. A life-sized picture of a girl in an old-fashioned brocade dress, with stiffly cushioned brown-gold hair, and a face which, although the colouring had grown yellow with time, still bore sufficient token of having been strikingly handsome. Some odd reflection from the candle at the present moment gave to the features a curiously cynical smile, while, as the light struck full upon the pictured form, it looked more substantial, more human, than the shadowy grey figure staring up at it.

As Hugh hesitated whether to speak or to go quietly away without making his presence known, Judy suddenly raised her arm; she clenched her fist, and shook it angrily at the placid, smiling face above her.

"You little—little—little—she-devil!" she hissed; then, disappearing into the room opposite, she slammed the door violently behind her.

> " For, in that thin frame,
> Pain-twisted,   .   .   .
> There lived a lavish soul until it starved,
> Debarred all healthy food."
>
> R. BROWNING.

CHAPTER IV.

SUNDAY, contrary to all reasonable expectations, dawned bright and warm. Higgins had his desire, and spent the morning, face downwards, on the grass. Over his head was a blue sky flecked with soft white clouds; around him a sunny sweep of country—green land and waving trees, yellow cornfields and shadowy hills melting into a colourless horizon. But Higgins gazed stolidly at the tangled grass beneath him. When his pipe was exhausted he plucked a round blade out of the ground and chewed it sleepily. His satisfaction was complete.

In the mean time his more conscientious superiors had betaken themselves to the village church, Sir Edward alone having remained at home, a martyr to gout.

Hugh had walked down the park that morning with Dick Thornton, his gaze riveted on the basket-chaise which was bearing Maud and Judy along the road before him. The black pony which drew the small carriage, and the tiny groom, who, as a light weight, adorned the back seat, were all that could be desired by the most critical taste; but, though a great improvement on what he had pictured to himself, Hugh eyed the neat equipage with disfavour. He felt vaguely relieved when it disappeared from sight over the brow of the hill.

The church lay about a mile from the house, and conversation did not flow very briskly between the two men on the way. Hugh was classifying his companion as a slow sort of a fellow who would have been marvellously brushed up by going into the army; and Dick Thornton, studying his cousin from time to time with a pair of shrewd brown eyes, was considering what a sorry figure such a self-opinionated, empty-headed chap would have cut at his own profession, the Bar, or indeed any profession which required brains. Thus, though bored with each other's society, it had at least the effect of promoting in them that spice of self-satisfaction which is conducive to a Christian frame of mind. We never feel so magnanimous and genially-disposed to the rest of mankind as at the moment when we are convinced of their distinct inferiority to ourselves.

The Lilcot family pew was an erection of worm-eaten woodwork, with high narrow seats cushioned in faded magenta; an oak table, also worm-eaten; eight extremely high magenta footstools, containing in their recesses a sufficient number of prayer-books and hymn-books to have liberally supplied the whole congregation; and a fireplace, which in winter was fed at appropriate intervals by the sexton, and in summer was decorated by his wife with a gaudy waterfall of white and rose paper.

Punctually at eleven the school-children clattered noisily into church; the last straggling remnants of the choir shuffled into their places;

Mr. Wilson—the tall, lean incumbent—appeared at the reading-desk, clad in a surplice which had been fashioned for his predecessor of exactly opposite height and proportions; and the service began.

Lilcot Church was decidedly behind the times in its appointments. The choir was composed of a judicious mixture of youths and maidens who had been chosen for the excellence of their morals rather than from any suspicion of musical talent. These vied with each other in shouting to the utmost limit of their unquestionably healthy lungs, and were supported by a shrilly nasal echo from the school-children at the other end of the building. The almost obsolete office of clerk was filled by the village shoemaker, who spouted the responses in a voice remarkable for its quaint pronunciation and supreme oblivion of the letter *h*. Mrs. Wilson, the rector's wife, presided at the organ, and quavered forth chants and hymns relieved by variations of her own, which occasionally threw the choir into confusion, and made the repre-

sentatives of village gentility look at each
other and smile patronizingly. But the very
primitiveness of everything was delightful to
Hugh. From his corner in the square pew he
viewed the humours of his surroundings with
keen interest, noting all the little eccentricities
which had once been so familiar to him, and
finding in this bit of the Past which was now
being re-enacted, much at once amusing and
pathetic in its homely simplicity.

The entrance door was left open, and the
breeze came wandering, warm and fragrant, up
the aisle. Stealing through the damp church, it
seemed laden with the hum of insects dancing
without in the sunshine, and with the scent of
flowers which were blooming there on the quiet
graves. At times the chirping of sparrows on
the church porch half drowned Mr. Wilson's
faint murmur of the prayers. The occasional
barking of a sheep-dog in the village broke
sharply upon the prevailing stillness.

Facing the congregation, Hugh studied and
re-studied them with decided curiosity. Were

the brief glances constantly directed towards
him by several members of the congregation
occasioned by the mere interest which the sight
of any stranger has for the bucolic mind, or did
they arise from a suspicion of his identity ? As
he ran his eye along the row of serious stolid
faces before him, a few of them slowly grew
familiar to him; he could here and there trace
resemblances to other and younger faces which
had, years ago, watched him from the same
points of observation. Now and then names
flashed to his memory like an inspiration ; the
people before him became like the small blocks
of a puzzle, which he fitted slowly, one by one,
into their places in his brain, till the whole
on a sudden assumed the form of a picture he
remembered well.

At last Mr. Wilson ascended the winding
steps of the pulpit to deliver his address. He
opened the Bible, stroked down its leaves with
reverent precision, cleared his throat several
successive times in a variety of keys, and,
having glanced severely round upon his con-

gregation, read out his text twice with the air
of a man who is stating a fact which he expects
to be immediately contradicted, and which he
is, at all costs, determined to maintain.

The congregation had settled themselves in
their pews with up-turned attentive faces.
Probably they did not anticipate gaining any
new ideas or receiving any soul-stirring benefit
from what they should hear. It was even possible they considered Mr. Wilson too learned
and too far above their unpretentious intellects
for such a result to be feasible. But there was
a satisfaction in the knowledge that some one
was anxious for their spiritual well-being, and
that they, on their part, were politely wishing
him every success in his kind efforts. To study
one's pastor's face with an unflinching stare was
a return-civility due from every good church-
going Christian.

Hugh, with his arms folded, sat stiffly upright
against the straight back of the family pew.
In his cool, well-fitting garments and spotless
collar and cuffs, he looked even more than

usually irreproachable. Dick, in the next
corner, staring absently up at the rafters over
his head, presented a marked contrast, with
rounded back, a face remarkable rather for its
look of shrewdness and determination than for
any more superficial attractions, and a shabby
brown coat, the creation of a village tailor.
Opposite was seated Maud, fast resigning herself to an overpowering sleepiness; her head
resting heavily against the oaken trellis-work,
crushing her flimsy pink bonnet amongst the
dark masses of her hair. In the other corner
sat Judy; a large brown hat tipped over her
eyes, her gaze fixed solemnly on the oak table
before her.

The air which now crept in at the open door
seemed to have become oppressively warm.
The twittering in the churchyard had grown
more sleepy; the sheep-dog was either basking
lazily in the hot sunshine, or had gone away to
attend to some of the serious business of life;
the hum of the insects grew louder, and seemed
to pervade the church with a continuous sing-

song, which mingled drowsily with Mr. Wilson's monotonous voice.

Hugh listened to the sermon. It was upon the Creation and the Fall. At least sixty million souls, Mr. Wilson affirmed, were born annually on the face of this earth. Add to these the innumerable tribes of brute and insect life which existed, calculate in what proportion to mankind they increased annually, then multiply the whole by the number of years the world had presumably existed, and it would give some faint conception of the consequences of Eve's disobedience. All these lives which had come into being since the creation of the world, all the lives which were yet to come into being during the possibly remote ages of the future, would have been sinless, painless, and ideally happy but for Eve's one fatal act.

Out of one of the windows of the chancel Hugh saw where the branches of a tree stirred languidly against a background of blue sky. Sixty million. He found himself wondering how many human beings had been born since he himself came into existence? Sixty million multiplied by thirty. Why, in thirty years alone that would make one thousand eight hundred million human creatures born to suffer and to die, because ages before a woman had succumbed to the childlike naughtiness of eating something 'good to the eye' which she had been told not to touch. In a hundred years how many people would have been punished? He tried to calculate. But the stirring branches at which he gazed seemed to confuse his thought. Now the branches looked blurred. Next the window grew suddenly dark. His eyes had closed.

With a start he roused himself, and glanced about him. No one had noticed his brief nap. He crossed his legs and sat more stiffly upright.

Now he turned his attention once more to the villagers. How had these people, he wondered, lived through their monotonous lives since he saw them last? What must it be to exist from year's end to year's end in one little isolated spot of the world ; to creep slowly from childhood to the fulness of life and vigour, thence to wander down the slope of old age into the grave waiting at its foot, without one vision, one desire beyond the line of their limited horizon ? Looking down at it from the pinnacle of a wider experience, how boring, how valueless, life under such conditions appeared ! Could it yield pleasure sufficient to be worth the mere daily fret of attention to the needs of the flesh—the wearisome daily routine of resting the body for a sufficient number of hours, of clothing it for active life, of feeding it at suitable intervals, of keeping it, its habiliments and its surroundings, in a state of cleanliness, of unclothing and resting it again after a few hours' work—could life, spent solely in the effort of sustaining itself, be worth that effort ?

Hugh yawned. Perhaps, to these uninitiated villagers, the daily round might seem as full of interest and of incident as was at all needful. The mind adapts itself to the groove in which

it must move, and what is life at the best but
a question of whiling away the time till death ?
Moreover, the most stirring elements of existence were known to them; pain, grief, love,
could visit them and sway their torpid natures.
But, as Dick had once justly remarked, all
the more subtle gradations of feeling, all the
finer and more exquisite stages of both pleasure
and suffering, must be unknown to them; they
could experience coarsely, powerfully, but the
thousand-and-one joys, needs, torments, which
go to make up the keen interest of living must
be impossible to them.

His gaze wandered to where Judy sat
crouched in a corner of the pew, with her large
hat tipped over her face. What could this
girl's experience of life be, more than the
yokel's? Save in superiority of education and
companionship—that is to say, the knowledge
of correct grammar, the society of a clique of
relations—her horizon must be narrower even
than that of the village folk. It struck him
now for the first time that the poorest village

girl, coarse, clumsy, ignorant, had, in com-
parison with Judy, her fair chance in the
lottery of life, the sweets of existence were
within her grasp, she had a share in the
pleasurable uncertainty of what good things
Fate held in store for her.

To Judy, dreams or longings for the future
must be unknown. What did life mean for
her now ? He would try to understand.
Whatever of beautiful or marvellous the world
beyond Lilcot might contain must be comparatively a dead letter to her ; she was shut off
even from the pleasures, the amusements which
this quiet country life might have afforded
her ; she could never taste the mere delightful
fulness of health and youth in which young
things can rejoice ; furthermore, no glamour
of romance could ever steal over her colourless life, no love could be hers which was not
principally the outcome of pity. Her present
must be grey and valueless ; no fascinating
May-be of the future could exist for her.

And yet—this was so surprising—she seemed

so unconscious of any pathos in her lot, so unsaddened by the shadow which lay heavily over her life. Trying to account for this, Hugh concluded that her very circumstances must have prevented her developing keen feelings. She might be said to exist rather than live, and, like the villagers, her sensitiveness had been blunted. Thus only could she be this merry flippant creature, with a certain superficial cleverness which found vent, as he had already discovered, in sharp cynical remarks, and odd, often unpleasant ideas, but whose capacity for pleasure and for pain, for longing, for regretting, was evidently deadened by the narrowing influence to which she had been subjected.

Judy pushed up her hat. The face which it had hidden was very serious now. Her eyes were still fixed upon the table before her. Did she think it right to choose some object in church at which to gaze in order to keep her attention from wandering? As Hugh watched, he acknowledged that he should not have suspected this serious side to her nature, and, still less, that Mr. Wilson's disjointed string of truisms would call it forth. But afflicted people were usually very religious. Hugh's Philosophy of Religion might have been expressed in the statement that a certain amount of happiness was needful to each human being, and that, when impossible through earthly sources, they sought it through spiritual.

At the very moment when he least expected it, Judy looked up as on the previous evening, and surprised his gaze fixed upon her. A faint flush crept over her face, and, with a look of annoyance, she turned away towards the congregation. Hugh felt vexed. Why, he asked himself, should she resent his chance scrutiny in so absurd a manner, or act as though she had any cause to be angry at it? Was it possible—he smiled—she could look upon it in the light of impertinent admiration? Certainly he had heard of instances where dwarfs and deformities had believed themselves to be indescribably fascinating. He could recall stories illustrative of this peculiar freak of Nature—the

'Theory of Compensation' he had heard it called. It was a comforting belief from one point of view; from another it might have its objections. He fixed his gaze on a wall in the aisle, and did not allow it to wander in the direction of the small figure opposite to him.

At last Mr. Wilson brought his remarks to a close. There was a sudden stir throughout the church, and the congregation, with a rustle of Sunday skirts, and a clatter of thick-soled Sunday boots, rose to their feet. Maud awoke from her slumbers and stared aimlessly about her; Judy slid down from her high hassock and began fumbling in her pocket in evident search of some coin loose in its depths. Then came a clink of pennies throughout the church. Mr. Wilson read the offertory sentences in a more animated voice, as though buoyed up by some vision of a savoury meal awaiting him in the rectory hard by; there was a brief hush while the congregation bent their knees and bowed their heads for the final blessing; then, noisily,

like children let loose from restraint, they began
clattering out of church.

It was the custom for the *élite* of the congregation to sit quietly in their pews while their
inferiors disappeared from the building, during
which time they avoided showing any remote
intention of following the common herd. It
would have been possible to gauge the exact
social status of any member of the community
by that individual's time and method of leaving
church on Sunday.   First, out hurried the
school-children and some ploughboys who usually
came late and sat near the door. Then followed
the unimportant bulk of the congregation—
village matrons anxious respecting the babies,
and the Sunday dinner left at home in inex-
perienced hands; farmers and labourers with
their thoughts on the ripened grain and the
state of the weather; girls in their Sunday
finery ready for a walk home with certain
sheepish-faced village lads who would be waiting for them in the churchyard; and a few old
folk who hobbled from the House of Worship

with lingering, regretful steps, unlike the hurry
of their busy neighbours. When these were
gone, Mrs. Knowle, the housekeeper from the
Hall, rose slowly from her seat, and stepped
away down the aisle with great dignity,
followed by three or four of the under-servants.
Miss Branberry, the village dressmaker, then
promptly grasped a lace parasol and emerged
from her pew, followed by her friend Miss
Greyson of the Co-operative, a village heiress.
Close behind them came Griggs, the bailiff of
the Lilcot estate, who strode away accompanied
by his portly wife, and followed by a large
assortment of little Griggses. Then Miss Brown,
a spinster of means who lived in a villa outside
the village, condescended to make her exit;
and, lastly, the little Wilsons were driven down
the aisle from their pew in the chancel by a
gaunt, severe-looking nurse.

Now the sexton, who had been holding the
door open, closed it, and sharply turned the key
in the lock as though he had a lurking fear that
the congregation might change their minds and

return; after which, slowly hobbling up the aisle, he made his way to a smaller door near the chancel and unbarred it. Judy, thereupon, rose; having pushed back the pew door, she slowly crossed the chancel, and, bowing gravely to the old sexton, passed out of the dim church into the brilliant sunshine.

The villagers had by now disappeared down the broad high-road leading from the church. Opposite the chancel door was a shady lane, which, sloping abruptly down the hill, formed a private way into the park below, and towards which ran a narrow path, winding in and out amongst the graves. Along this Judy paced solemnly, and was joined by Dick Thornton.

Hugh found himself beside Maud.

"Are you going to walk home?" he asked.

"Judy always drives to church and walks back," said Maud, regretfully. "It is a bad arrangement, as now it is the hottest time of day, and one feels lazy."

"Isn't it rather far for her to walk?" Hugh

lowered his voice, for they were overtaking the pair in front.

"Yes, Mr. Wilson always uses Providence as a convenient scapegoat," Judy was saying as they passed.

Maud waited to reach the lane before she answered.

"Judy can do a good bit, provided she does not go too fast and overtire herself. But she is very unequal. Some days she can do much more than others. Some days, of course, she suffers more than others."

Hugh hit a stone with his cane. It bounded down the hill, and he watched it absently.

"You think she does suffer?" he remarked after a pause.

Maud looked at him reflectively. Then she turned to pluck some sweetbriar from the hedge, and arranged it leisurely in her white dress.

"Of course she suffers, poor child, mentally and physically." She looked at his face again. "Hugh!" she said suddenly, "I want to give you a hint. You used to be a kind-hearted fellow, and you might do a great deal for her, and be a great deal to her, but I feel you two are really total strangers now, and she is not easy to make friends with. Therefore I want to impress upon you—don't judge her superficially, or you will be likely to misunderstand her; and if you want to win her good will, you had better ignore the fact of her not being like other people. Never make any allusions to her health, and never show that you notice anything unusual in her appearance."

" You really consider this advisable?"

" I am certain of it!" Maud answered quickly. " If you notice, you will find Uncle Edward has much the same peculiarity. His one hobby is to deceive himself and to blind others with regard to Judy's deformity. He will go the most preposterous lengths and make the most absurd statements in his endeavour to do this, and it is really a great kindness to humour him as far as lies in one's power. With Judy the same mania arises, partly from a desire to spare her father's feelings, and partly from a morbid

dread of being pitied. You will probably discover this as you get to know her better, but
it might not strike you at first."

Hugh looked thoughtful.

"No, I can't say she appeared to me either
morbid or sensitive," he remarked.

"Probably not." Maud spoke dryly. "I
have noticed there is many a fact in this world
which never would strike men unless some
woman took the trouble to point it out to
them."

A short silence ensued, broken by a sudden
fear on Hugh's part that their conversation
might have been overheard by those behind.
He glanced back uneasily, and discovered that
Dick was sauntering after them alone.

"Where is Judy?" he exclaimed.

Maud looked lazily round.

"She has gone back to the churchyard, I
expect. A little boy belonging to her Sunday
school class died not long since, and I believe
she promised him to put flowers on his grave
weekly. At any rate, she usually does so on

Sunday morning after church, and I imagine she has gone back there now."

" Then does she walk home by herself ? "

" As a rule."

Hugh tapped his boots with his stick, and watched the little sprinkling of dust which fell from them.

" Shall I go back and look for her ? " he asked at length.

" It is not necessary."

" Perhaps it isn't good for her to be much alone ? "

" Perhaps not."

Hugh tapped his boots more energetically.

" If you think of going back," said Maud, " why don't you go ? "

Without another word he turned and strode rapidly away up the hill.

"Thou art a little soul bearing about a corpse, as Epictetus used to say."—M. AURELIUS ANTONINUS.

CHAPTER V.

THE wind blew softly in Hugh's face as he emerged from the lane. It was a warm wind, but it stirred refreshingly among the hedges near at hand, making the small dry leaves quiver upon their stems. He paused, partly to inhale this faint breath of air, partly from an unacknowledged reluctance to proceed. Would Judy be annoyed at his returning? Maud had surely implied it might be so, and that she preferred her own society? Therefore would he not have been wiser to have returned home with the rest of the party? For one moment he sought about in his mind for some plausible excuse for retracing his steps; then, with an unaccountable feeling of shyness, he began peering about the churchyard for some glimpse

of Judy's brown hat and dust-coloured dress.
Any fear which might have been present in
his mind of her possibly misconstruing this
little token of brotherly good-nature on his
part had been rendered impossible by the
new light in which her character had been
represented to him by Maud; he felt a certain
shame at the thoughts which had come to him
in church; no doubt, while he had been credit-
ing her with amusing conceit and affectation,
the poor girl had been shrinking from his gaze
in sheer humiliation. He felt angry with
himself, and his heart was full of a desire to
atone for having thus misjudged and insulted
her in his secret thoughts.

He stepped on to the little path and moved
slowly along it. Slanting weather-stained
tombstones stood on either side, half blocking
out the view. The place was very still. The
organ no longer sounded noisily through the
open door. Mr. and Mrs. Wilson had gone
home to their well-earned midday meal; the
sexton had locked up the chancel, and departed

to his cottage in the village. The little hill-side was deserted.

Hugh gained the broad road before the church. Here the sun blazed down upon the white flags. The faint breath of wind had died away. In the long-branched ivy over the porch a bird stirred, chirping lazily as though in resentment at his intrusion.

He looked away to the distance. At the bend of the road the village lay asleep in the hot sunshine. The cool meadows sloping down to it were gold and white with flowers. Beyond, in shadowy background, stretched the line of dim grey hills.

Hugh felt a strange oppression in the sleepy scene. As far as eye could reach no human being was in sight. The dreamy hush was unbroken. Only the stir of insect-life made a murmur in the air. He was alone with the dead in a world where the living were asleep. He shaded his eyes from the sun and drew a deep breath. There was a stupefying influence in the heat.

Yet he remained gazing at the long stretch of land before him with an expression of marked solemnity. The thought had come to him that all this peaceful country lying mapped out at his feet would one day be his own absolutely, to make or to mar as he chose. He was bound to it by a peculiar tie ; till death his fate was indissolubly linked with it. Gradually the petty misgivings which a moment before had troubled him, even the remembrance of what had brought him back into this solitude, passed from him. He stroked his moustache complacently. He was experiencing a drowsy satisfaction in his own importance, a sleepy consciousness of his power and worth.

Suddenly a voice broke rudely upon his meditations.

" What, in the name of goodness, did you come back to look for ? " it asked. " Did you leave your wits in church ? "

With a start Hugh looked round to discover Judy standing a little distance off, among the tombstones, watching him. There was a sus-

picion of a smile upon her face. To his annoyance, he felt he was blushing scarlet. He had
an uncomfortable conviction that she had been
watching him for some moments, and that,
soliloquizing thus upon the hill-top, he must
have cut a supremely ridiculous figure.

Gathering his scattered thoughts, he tried to
speak in a tone of easy indifference.

"I have come to walk home with you," he said.

"Oh!"

It seemed to him there was a world of meaning in Judy's voice. Again he wished he had
gone sensibly home with the saner members
of his family.

She was coming towards him now, every few
moments disappearing behind some tall tomb-
stone, then threading her way in the narrow
spaces between the graves. Hugh strolled to
meet her. As he stepped upon the grass, she
was still a few yards distant, and suddenly she
waved to him excitedly.

"Take care!" she cried hurriedly. "You
are treading on a grave!"

Hugh sprang aside almost before he had realized what she said. Then he laughed at himself for having done so.

"Are you superstitious?" he asked, hoping she would notice the slight sarcasm he introduced into his voice.

"Not a bit!" Judy answered disdainfully. "But"—looking up into his face and speaking in a whisper—"if you were lying voiceless down there, wouldn't you hate being trampled underfoot by the lucky living?"

She was standing beside him now, and Hugh looked at her with mingled curiosity and misgiving. Was the sudden awe which had crept into her voice serious or facetious? He was anxious not to commit himself.

"I probably should not know much about it," he suggested cautiously, though aware the remark was not strikingly original.

Judy nodded her head solemnly.

"Possibly," she acquiesced; "but, all the same, isn't it difficult to realize that the dead have no more of humanity left in them now

than the mould in which they lie?" She cast
her eyes slowly over the graves by which she
was surrounded. "When I was a child I read
that story of Hans Andersen in which he
describes the old man lying, dumb and forgotten, in his grave, listening to the talk of
the children who were playing over him in
the sunshine; and, since then, I have never
been able to think of the people in these graves
otherwise than as being afflicted with a terrible powerlessness to speak or stir, but keenly
capable of thought and suffering, and it seemed
to me that the worst form that suffering must
take must be to lie quiet there and know that
overhead the sun is shining, and the busy
world going on as though one had never formed
part of it. I think"—Judy's eyes flashed—
"it would madden me with jealousy!"

Hugh felt hopelessly perplexed. One point
only was clear to him—the conversation was
drifting into an unpleasant channel, and he
must turn it in some other direction. Before
he could speak, however, Judy pointed to the

headstone of the grave on which he had stepped.

" Do you remember old Benjamin Jones, the gamekeeper?" she asked. "That is his grave. You used to be so fond of him in old days, and always at his heels. He died quite suddenly in a fit two years ago. I was dreadfully sorry about it. That little grave near is a small grand-child of his who died about the same time."

"Just fancy poor old Jones being gone!" said Hugh. "I had forgotten about it, and had been meaning to ask you if we couldn't go up to the kennels to see him this afternoon. Poor old chap! I feel as if the place wouldn't be the same without him."

" That grave over there," said Judy, pointing to one a little way off, "is Mrs. Broadbent's. Do you remember the lovely teas she used to give us at the lodge ; and the gingerbread-nuts she used to cram into our pockets behind Fräu-lein's back? She died of cancer last year, poor thing! I believe she suffered agonies first."

" What a lot of the old friends seem gone!"

observed Hugh, experiencing an increasing desire to get Judy out of the churchyard.

She seemed, however, to find a distinct enjoyment in her present conversation. Strolling on a few paces, she pointed out another grave.

" I expect you remember that little fellow ? " she said; " Ned Taylor's son. A very bright, intelligent boy you took a great fancy to. He died of rapid consumption; and, it is so sad, they say the girl is going just the same, and she is the only child they have left. I suppose she will soon be buried next him."

To Hugh's relief, she began walking towards the lane; but in another moment her eye fell upon a grave to the right, marked by a plain white cross, and again she paused.

" That girl has an odd story," she said. " Probably you may hear it mentioned, so I will put you *au fait* of the scandal; then you need ask no questions."

She made her way to the grave, and, leaning one arm against the cross, looked down at the inscription, whose black letters cut the gleaming surface of the marble in clear, sharp lines.

'ALINE DAVIES,

died

July 12th, 18—.

Aged seventeen years.'

Beneath was a verse—

"We have drunken of Lethe at last, we have eaten of
    lotus;
  What hurts it us here that sorrows arise and die?
  We have said to the dream that caressed and the terror
    that smote us,
        Good-night and good-bye."

Judy followed Hugh's gaze.

"Don't ask me if that is a hymn," she said quickly. "It is Swinburne. It was put there at my special request, because it so exactly suited the girl's story. Listen. Soon after you went away, the man who owned the Cedar Farm, halfway between here and Cranthorpe, left, and a Mr. Davies, a rich farmer, came to live there. He had one daughter, a lovely girl. I think I have never seen any one so pretty before or since. She had hair like thick shimmering gold "—Judy's voice waxed enthusiastic—"a face like a wild rose, and great violet eyes with long curling lashes. Her beauty was of a very uncommon type. When we had people staying with us, we used often to make some excuse to call at the farm that they might see her. Well, young Bob Grafton, Lord Ellington's son, fell in love with her. She was then only sixteen. He used to make endless excuses to ride over to the farm, and spent half his days watching pretty Allie making butter, feeding chickens, or wandering in the old orchard to pick up the fallen apples. The old farmer was safe at his work, and Allie had no mother at home to interfere with any tiresome caution. It must have been a charming romance! But, unfortunately, Bob was not noted for being too scrupulous. He became too much in love for prudence, and tried to persuade Aline to go away with him. I don't mean marry him," explained Judy, apologetically—"just go off with him. No doubt the girl's head had been full of brilliant dreams of one day being Lady Ellington, with jewels and servants and carriages of her own; but, beyond all this, she had grown to care for him deeply. The shock of discovering the kind of love he bore her was probably terrible. Yet still the tragedy went on without any one suspecting, he bullying her, she growing to care more and more. All this while she was becoming paler, her eyes looked larger and more lovely; people said she was more refined—prettier than before. Then came the end. A labourer, walking through the park at home early one morning, discovered her dead in the lake. It was said she had met her lover on the hillside the evening before, and walked with him for the last time. But, however that may be, she had left a note for her father, saying she intended to drown herself, because she had grown to love young Grafton so intensely she knew she was powerless to resist his influence much longer, and had therefore decided upon the only course to save herself from sin." Judy looked down

at the grave again. " The villagers would tell
you that, on moonlight nights, her spirit still
haunts the hillside where she last walked with
her lover. You see, the story caused a great
sensation in the place. Young Grafton left
home till it should have blown over, and he is
engaged to a girl in London now—a 'nice
marriage,' his people say."

A big golden butterfly came floating lazily
over the primulas which bordered the grave.
Hugh touched it with his stick, and it fluttered
away.

" What a tragic little history!" he said. " I
can imagine how it would stir up this sleepy
hollow. Awkward for Bob Grafton if his 'nice'
wife gets to hear of it! It was rather rough on
him, the girl making such a public scandal of
the affair. The moral of poor Aline's story
seems to be—don't flirt with girls of sixteen,
they're too romantic!"

Judy stooped down and poked with her finger
at a nettle growing near the white cross. She
bent it cautiously over, grasped its stem, and

pulled it up by the roots; then, flinging it away on to the path, she looked up.

" Do you consider the girl was wrong to drown herself?" she asked.

" Why—of course!" answered Hugh, surprised at the question. " As wrong as foolish. But I suppose people can love like that at sixteen. I believe even I used to do so!" He laughed lightly. " Though, in cases of this sort, I'm certain a girl often acts more out of reckless temper than anything else. She wants to pay the man out by letting the world know how he has treated her, and she succeeds admirably!"

Judy rose and looked at him, her forehead drawn into a slight frown.

" Listen!" she said. " Though it seems quaintly humorous that any one could drown themselves for love of a Bob Grafton, yet, don't you grasp that the exact reason of Aline's act was to save herself from feelings which were overpowering her? She drowned herself because she recognized it was the sole escape from wrong possible to her."

Hugh smiled.

" What business had she to let her feelings run away with her to such an extent ? "

" Could she help it ? "

Hugh shrugged his shoulders.

" Where should any of us be without a little self-control and common sense in life ? "

" Self-control is simple for a shallow nature."

The look of amusement upon Hugh's face deepened.

" Don't you feel," he suggested, " as if your heroine might be eavesdropping? Would it not be wiser if we moved further away ? "

Judy tossed back her hat.

" We don't have luncheon till two o'clock, if that is what you mean," she retorted, and began moving away towards the lane.

Hugh, following her, watched her furtively with considerable amusement. He fancied, in the occasional glimpses he caught of her face, that it bore a sulky expression. She had been, for once, talking seriously, and was evidently annoyed with him for his flippant interruption.

What a strange girl she was! he reflected; so changeable, and utterly unaccountable in her different moods; so obstinate and argumentative, with her head full of odd fancies and theories. The conversation just now had been flavoured with a strong spice of originality, and had been unlike what he would have had with any ordinary girl. The Judy of To-day was an interesting phenomenon.

As they entered the lane side by side, he looked at her once more. Walking downhill made her deformity more apparent. Her head seemed to jerk slightly backwards and forwards with every step she took. Her shoulders swayed unpleasantly. Soon he looked away.

After a few moments, he felt rather than saw that she turned to him with that quick observant glance which had been habitual to her as a child.

"I don't think," she remarked, "that church-yards appeal to you as they do to me?"

"I fancy not," answered Hugh, briefly.

"Now, they appeal to me very strongly,"

continued Judy, confidentially. "There is something so specially fascinating in prowling amongst those little green mounds, and trying to realize that they each mark some effaced human life, some evaporated existence. One tries to imagine all the sorrows, the torments, the dreams, which those cold sods of earth have fastened down into mysterious silence. Funerals, of course, appeal to me, too. It seems to me as though all living creatures must feel as I do on this subject; for death is so odd—its incomprehensibility fascinates one."

"You mean like ghost-stories?" suggested Hugh—"give one a creepy-crawly sensation."

"I hate ghost-stories!" interrupted Judy, vehemently. "I hate the idea that, after death, people take a malicious pleasure in returning to play poor practical jokes on the living! My liking for churchyards and corpses is different." She paused, as though puzzled how to express her meaning, then went on rapidly. "It is a love of the extraordinary. Just think! an insignificant bit of lead sent into you, a piece of hemp drawn too tightly round your neck, the mere prick of a needle in some vital spot, and you could be thereby changed into a senseless mummy, rigid and grim, which, after passing through several unprepossessing stages of decomposition, would crumble into ordinary mould. It is so queer!"

Yes, Maud was right in thinking her morbid. Hugh reflected that, in the *rôle* of fatherly monitor to Judy which he had secretly taken upon himself, he ought to check this tendency.

"You really should not let your mind dwell upon such unpleasant subjects; it is bad for you," he ventured mildly.

"That is a very commonplace view to take of the matter," said Judy, loftily. "You miss the interest in these thoughts because you don't realize their application to yourself. Do you know, as a matter of fact, we are all inclined to look upon the dead as a distinct species from ourselves? We stare at a corpse with a feeling of unconscious contempt. We think, 'Poor thing! here am I still clever enough to walk, and talk, and fend for myself. You aren't capable of all this now; you are going to be nailed into a box and hurried out of sight, because you are useless and no longer intelligent.' But we never realize we shall one day be just the same. We *know* it, of course, but the warm life in our veins denies it roundly; we try to grasp the fact, and then it is that the fascination comes in. How odd! How incomprehensible! One day we too shall be *that!* What will it be like? What can it all mean?"

She glanced at Hugh and noted the expression of his face.

" We are all afraid of death—yes," she added, with the air of one who is making a great concession, " but that is because the Unknown may mean pain from which we have a natural shrinking; but the mysteriousness of the Unknown has none the less its peculiar fascination, and the more awesome, the more gruesome, the greater the fascination!"

Hugh felt growing rapidly more and more

bewildered. He took refuge in a feeble reiteration of his former remark.

"Merely the ordinary vulgar love of the creepy-crawly," he murmured.

"No, it isn't!" said Judy, hotly. "You don't understand." Then a mischievous expression stole over her face, and the corners of her mouth curled into a smile. "Life is much more creepy! Go to the Albert Hall when it is packed with people, as I did on one eventful day of my existence, and sit in some seats high up; then, after you have been well saturated by the music, churned up into an ideal, ethereal, poetical state of feeling, come back with a rush to the realism of life and watch the crowd disperse. Look at the black struggling mass of creatures down in the distance"— Judy pointed and waved her hand before her—" look at that moving, heaving crowd! Do you see how they swarm backwards and forwards, how they collect together in wriggling groups, how they separate into thin straggling lines? They are like crawling insects! The place is alive with them! Phew! Is there nothing creepy in the sight? To me it brings a sense of disgust." She looked again into Hugh's face. "The study of an isolated personality is wonderful—exciting; the sight of life in a swarming animal mass is loathsome!"

Was the girl's brain maimed as well as her body?—Hugh pondered. Was she merely talking for effect, and trying to impress him with would-be cleverness? Or was all her conversation an endeavour to get some fun out of him?

They had reached the foot of the hill where a narrow stream—an offshoot from the water in the park—crossed the road. The stream was shallow, and while Hugh made use of the clumsy little bridge, Judy preferred to skip from stone to stone through the water, splashing herself plentifully, and sliding awkwardly on the wet pebbles. As they turned into the park, she resumed the conversation.

"I was thinking about it in church to-day," she continued. "Mr. Wilson kept on discussing

the different types of life, you know; and I
began studying the wood-lice. That old oak
table in the pew swarms with them, and they
are such queer little imitations of the larger
forms of life. Don't you know how they
scurry about, so fussed, anxious, and busy, till
one wonders what their lives mean to them?
Why they fret and fidget in that inane manner?
What they imagine their aimless fuss and
activity is accomplishing—these absurd little
atoms in a crowded world? Oh, types are
interesting; it is when life in a big mass is
thrust too obtrusively under one's notice that
it becomes objectionable. When it is forced
upon one that not only every available square
inch around one is teeming with it, but that
every living organism represents a habitation
for lesser developments of it, and so on"—
again her eyes twinkled—"there is something
not only oppressive, but actively creepy to my
mind."

Hugh pulled his cigar-case out of his pocket
and held it meditatively in his hand.

" Do you object to smoking ? " he asked.

Judy shook her head impatiently, and he proceeded to strike a match. Shielding the little red flame with his hands, he stood drawing it up into the tobacco till the tip of the cigar glowed like a pale ember. Then he flung the match away and walked on, sending thin wreaths of silver smoke out into the sunshine.

" Well," he remarked at length, holding his cigar between his finger and his thumb, " you have the most unpleasant ideas of any one I ever came across ! "

Judy had been watching him with bright expectant eyes; now her face suddenly fell. She turned her head quickly away.

" Why won't you understand," she said pettishly, " that it is not the nastiness of life I appreciate, but the queerness of life ? However, you think otherwise. Let us talk of something else."

There followed an interval of complete silence. They strolled slowly on through the long cool grass. Here, under the wide trees, it was possible to pass from one deep shadow to another with only brief spaces of sunshine to traverse. The air was touched with a coldness from the waters of the lake.

Why, Hugh was now pondering, did conversation with his present companion always come to an untimely end? It consisted for the most part, certainly, of a running fire of extraordinary theories and arguments which were impossible to follow, and which could scarcely be dignified by the name of conversation; yet, directly she ceased to sustain it, it flagged. With other girls he found so many topics for discussion —tennis, dancing, society in general, mutual society acquaintances. With Judy these subjects were of necessity out of the question; the only topic he felt they must have in common— reminiscences of former friends and of former days—seemed to carry with it something too painful to be lightly handled.

Suddenly Judy spoke again.

"How do you think father is looking?" she inquired, with a certain studied politeness in the tone of her voice, as though she were anxious to atone for any little show of temper into which she had been betrayed.

Hugh, also labouring under an impression that they had in some inexplicable manner nearly approached a quarrel, conquered his dislike to turning in her direction, and, looking down at her, amiably answered in his most cordial tone—

"Marvellously well! He strikes me as more grey than ten years ago, otherwise I should notice comparatively little difference."

"You know he is anxious you should sell out and settle down here now?"

Hugh tapped his cigar with his finger, so that the grey ashes fell from it.

"That means marrying, in point of fact, and I understand there are good reasons for his wishing that; but I fear I am scarcely the man to so sacrifice myself! How is the family black sheep, Judy?"

There was a slight hesitation in Hugh's voice for which Judy was at no loss to account.

Whereas Sir Edward and his second brother, Hugh's father, had, in the various situations of life, acquitted themselves in a blameless and unremarkable manner, the youngest brother had launched forth into a more noticeable career. From college up to middle age his progress through existence had been marked by a series of scandals; his name, seldom mentioned in the Lilcot family, was openly discussed elsewhere in connection with racing, gambling, various shady money transactions, and stories which lent it a far from creditable notoriety. At first he had been a man in all the fastest and most fashionable set in town, but soon even the most reckless of his contemporaries began to look upon him doubtfully. Gradually they turned the cold shoulder upon him, and he dropped into a species of society vagrant. At the present time he was leading an uneventful life abroad, existing on blackmail levied from Sir Edward in the form of an annuity payable so long as he absented himself from his native shores. But, in the event of Hugh dying childless, he was

the next heir to the Lilcot estate, and the possibility of his coming into possession was viewed
with horror by all who had any interest in the
matter. Sir Edward himself had had visions
of Lilcot shunned by the rest of the county, of
the park denuded of its fine old trees to fill a
spendthrift's pockets, of neglected tenants and
damaged property, till he entertained serious
thoughts of attempting to buy his brother out
of the entail.

Judy laughed as she answered—

"Uncle Tom is growing rather decrepit, I
believe. I assure you, father is quite cheerful
on the subject! Now and then he has suggested
a visit here, but it is never likely to come off."
She looked at Hugh and hesitated. "I wonder
if it would be better to tell you something?"
she said doubtfully.

"Well?" said Hugh.

Judy gazed up at the sky with an expression
of profound interest.

"It will rain before night, I am certain."

Hugh did not consider it necessary to pretend

any keen interest in this prophetic remark.
Taking refuge in his cigar, he strolled on,
speculating aimlessly on what information Judy
had been about to vouchsafe when she had
changed her mind thus suddenly. Something
in connection with Tom Lilcot, he decided, and,
if so, doubtless unpleasant. He had an un-
describable dislike to even mentioning the man
who had disgraced the family name.

They turned off the grass, and, having
followed the winding carriage-drive for a few
yards, passed through a small iron gate into the
grounds. These were old-fashioned and quaint,
with beds of great rhododendron bushes looking
purple-black in the sunlight, drooping pale
laburnum trees, stiff acacias and clipt yews,
willows arched into delicate green tents with
rustic seats beneath them, and, between the
beds, wide spaces of smooth turf so thick with
moss that no footfalls could be heard upon it.
The hush of the hot noontide seemed once
more oppressive, and Hugh found himself
missing the rustle which Judy's skirts had made

as they swept over the long grass in the park.

Soon they saw Sir Edward coming slowly towards them down one of the trim gravel paths. He was a fine old man, tall and broad-chested. His white hair, the black velvet coat and wide felt hat which he wore, combined to give him a picturesque appearance. He turned back with them, and, walking still more slowly on account of his temporary lameness, they made their way to the house.

In front of the drawing-room window Hugh paused.

"Is it quite luncheon-time?" he asked.

Sir Edward consulted a ponderous gold watch.

"Ten minutes yet," he announced.

"Then I think I will just finish my cigar," said Hugh; and Sir Edward went on into the house.

Judy walked up to one of the window-sills and fetched a bit of stale bread which was lying there.

"I'm going to feed my pheasants," she said;

"but you mustn't come, Hugh, because they don't know you, and they won't come near me if you are there."

She walked off briskly towards the north side of the house, and Hugh strolled leisurely along the terrace. Soon he bent his steps in the direction of some trees at the foot of the lawn; the sunshine, tinting their foliage a brighter green, could only touch the grass beneath in soft mottled light and shadow. He paced to and fro in the grateful shade, occasionally glancing up to the green slope beyond the house where Judy's light dress showed from time to time amongst the bushes. Once he paused in his walk to watch it, and a smile passed over his face ; then he paced on, and his thoughts must have wandered into some other channel, for he did not glance again in the direction of the green slope.

Amongst the bushes Judy stood sprinkling bits of bread down through the wire. First she looked at the pheasants, then away at the lawn below, where Hugh strolled to and fro.

Her forehead was contracted into the same puzzled frown it had borne a short time before in the churchyard.

At last she gave vent to the result of her reflections.

"He is a fool!" she said emphatically, rubbing some bread vigorously between her hands. "A thorough-going, commonplace, matter-of-fact, irritating, uninteresting fool!"

And she looked anxiously at the cock-pheasant as though daring him to dispute her collection of adjectives. But the bird's intellect was not proof against unexpected good fortune —in the shape of bread-crumbs—which had been showered upon him. He was busily occupied eating his fastest, and trying to prevent the hens getting any fragments which it might be possible for him to appropriate personally.

Judy threw the crust far into the bushes and turned back to the house.

"See, when the lake is serene, how the whole mountain lies reflected in it, from base to summit, and with all its forests. Not a leaf is lost. The tree below stands there in that lower sky, in as calm an azure as the tree above. But the smallest pebble—and any hand can throw one; but the merest straw or withered leaf—and any idle wind may fling them there—shall blot out mountain and sky at once."—Thorndale.

CHAPTER VI.

SIR EDWARD was busy over his accounts. Judging by the untidy litter of papers with which he was surrounded, a long morning's work lay before him. The striped red blinds drawn over the windows to keep out the sun shed a subdued light through the large comfortable library with its book-covered walls. The only sound audible was the mingled ticking of the clock on the mantelpiece and the scratching of his pen as it moved rapidly over the paper.

The door opened softly.

"Is that you, Beales?" said Sir Edward, without looking up from the paper.

There was no answer. Then he felt an arm round his neck and a warm cheek laid against his.

"It isn't Beales, dad," said Judy; "and how you can think of accounts in this weather passes my comprehension!"

Sir Edward laid down his pen and looked at her over the top of his gold-rimmed glasses. Then he put his arm round her and pressed her cheek lightly against his own. The eyes in both faces were curiously alike, but while Judy's mouth suggested decision amounting to obstinacy, in Sir Edward's the flexible curve of the unclosed lips seemed to indicate a vacillation of purpose, an amiability bordering on weakness.

"What business has a frivolous creature like you to interrupt my morning's work?" he said.

"It is good for you to be interrupted, dad," said Judy. "I brought you a letter from Aline. I thought you would like to see it, as it gives rather an amusing account of their doings. The Daltons are probably going away to-morrow, so I suppose we shall shortly bask in the light of her countenance."

She placed a letter in his hand, and, disengaging herself from his arm, walked to the window and drew the blind up a little way, so that more light came into the room.

Sir Edward rearranged his glasses, and began perusing the note she had given him. At intervals he made little comments.

" Hum—ha—what a bad hand the girl writes ! What is that word?—times? terms? Oh, tennis! Spelt it with one ' n.' People used to learn to spell in my day ! Well," as he neared the end, " Dalton seems to know how to amuse his guests ! " Then he folded it up and held it out to Judy. " She will find us very quiet folk, after all the fun she has been having."

Judy took the letter, tore it across the middle, and stood diminishing it into smaller and smaller pieces.

" Has Hugh settled to stay here ? " she asked.

Sir Edward pushed his papers away with a sudden show of interest and rested his arm upon the table.

" We had a talk on the subject of his selling

out last night," he said. "I think he will probably go back to India for a year and then come home to settle down."

" If that is the case I shall not be alone," said Judy.

" And what then ? " asked Sir Edward.

Judy swept the fragments of the letter into one hand and threw them into the waste-paper basket.

" Simply this," she said energetically ; " it practically decides what we were discussing the other night. The case in point lies in a nut-shell. Aline's Scotch aunt, finding life dull without a companion, has asked her to go back to live in Edinburgh. Aline is willing—in fact, wishes to do so." Judy's lip curled. " The society of retired shopkeepers in Edinburgh is preferable to the absence of society at Lilcot. Moreover, her aunt proposes to travel. In short, she merely hesitates about accepting it from a feeling of gratitude—— "

" I never wish her to feel herself under any obligation to me," interrupted Sir Edward, gently; "anything I have done for her was merely my duty."

"Where, then, is the sense of her staying here to bore and be bored?" exclaimed Judy. "Patience me, daddy! if you knew what you had inflicted on me when you gave me that wholesome 'companionship of my own age—warranted cheerful,' which the aunts all told you I must require! I try to believe that the disagreeables of life are blessings in disguise, but some blessings are so cleverly disguised! Nell's society comes under that category. Imagine what it means to be asked a dozen times a day whether a fringe looks prettier curled up or down; whether blue, or brown, or pale tan is most becoming; whether a sash tied round the waist enlarges the figure, or whether, if properly tied, it makes it look smaller! It seems to me I have been discussing these vital questions daily for eight years. My overtaxed brain must have a holiday. Let Nellie accept a good offer now, while she has the chance, for it may not be renewed later, however much we wished

it.   Even you will be satisfied I do not require
more 'cheerful companionship' when Hugh
comes to live here."

Sir Edward laughed softly.   Judy's down-
right statements always afforded him keen
amusement.   His own remarks were apt to be
a gentle echo of the ideas which had just been
presented to himself.

"I should not have liked any thought of
getting rid of her," he said, "but, if she has a
chance of a good home elsewhere, it would, as
you say, be well for her to accept it.   The girl's
aunt has certainly as much claim on her as I
have.   Then, too, as you say, you will not need
her when Hugh is established here."

"I never did need her," muttered Judy,
"unless as a refining trial."

Sir Edward did not catch the remark.

"Yes, when Hugh comes home it will be
different," he repeated, as though trying to
assure himself of this fact.

Then he gave an unconscious sigh.   Was he
thinking of what might have been possible

when Hugh came home if the Fates had been less cruel to Judy?

Perhaps Judy heard the sigh, for she put her arm again swiftly about his neck and laid her brown head against his white locks.

" What a nice year we shall have together— you and I, dad!   Let us shut up the house, and say your gout is too bad to have any relations here!"

Sir Edward's face brightened.   There was a very tender light in the brown eyes which were looking into his own.   He pressed his lips against the soft hair.   The sunlight burnished it into fine glittering threads of spun fire and gold.

A heavy knock came at the door.   Judy lifted her head and moved quickly away.   She left the room as Beales, the gamekeeper, entered it.

Sir Edward had not heard the knock, and remained looking at his accounts with an absent smile.

" A happy little soul!" he observed aloud; then, with a touch of asperity in his voice

which made it sound oddly like Judy's firm
decisive tones, he added emphatically, " I say,
a particularly happy little soul ! "

Hugh came slowly walking up the park. He
had been villaging, but had taken his gun with
him for the chance of a stray pop at the rabbits
on his way back, and now he already carried
two victims of his prowess dangling limply by
their hind legs. He was thinking over the
enthusiastic welcome he had received from a
few of the old dames whom he had honoured
with his presence. What a tremendous event
his return was in their quiet lives! It was
pleasant to be the object of so much enthusiasm
and devotion, but was the future of his existence to begin and end with thus playing the
demigod to a set of faithful, boring rustics?
The *rôle* of country squire might seem truly
peaceable and enviable, but it closely resembled
the *rôle* in life filled by a healthy well-tended
vegetable. How dead-alive, how exasperatingly
placid, it might be ! A round of meals separated

by intervals of wondering whether last night's frost had nipped the fruit blossoms, whether yesterday's rain had injured the corn, whether old Croker had yet succumbed to the complaint which was so long removing him to a Better Land, whether Mrs. Yokel had yet presented the world with the expected addition to her voluminous family.

Though fully realizing its many advantages, he did not feel it a prospect which particularly elated him. His conversation with Sir Edward and the conclusion thereby arrived at was weighing upon him. How should he settle down into this vegetating existence now while he was young, and competent to enjoy life with the best? The dreamy hush of the country in this fine August weather was delightful; but to imagine existence one monotonous continuation of such drowsy perfection, instantly detracted from its charm. As a boy home for the holidays, life at Lilcot had appeared to him the realization of a very paradise on earth; now, as a place in which to spend a six months'

leave, it struck him as a charmingly easy-going,
lazy mode of existence. But he did not blind
himself to the fact that what was delightful
as a temporary state of being, would be the
reverse as a permanency. Sport appealed
to him as much as formerly—fishing, shooting,
hunting, had lost none of the charm they possessed for him as a boy ; but he knew that, apart
from these, the solitude and the want of incident
in country life would oppress him now as it had
never done then. He had been here but a short
time, and already he acknowledged to himself
his appreciation of it was waning. The pure-
ness of the air no longer gave him such keen
satisfaction ; the sweet, warm scents of earth,
wood, and blossom seemed less apparent; he
found himself remarking, instead, how uneventful the days were, how depressing this eternal
stillness of the country, how absolute the need
for congenial companionship.

He was wandering home for tea now. It
would be on the lawn. Maud, Judy, and
Dick, he told himself, would be keeping up a

running discussion on some irritating subject. Afterwards would come a long sleepy interval of doing nothing till dinner-time ; then, a meal enlivened only by a lengthy repetition of the conversation at tea, and by tedious stories of former days from Sir Edward; lastly, there would be the uneventful evening, Maud and Judy each buried in their books, Sir Edward asleep over the daily papers which arrived by the second post, Dick enjoying a quiet pipe on the terrace. So much for the present. How should he endure a perpetuation of this life with an old man and an invalid girl ?

"I must do my best to wake them up a bit," he reflected ruefully, " but it won't be easy work ; and, whenever I can, I shall get away to town."

The sound of voices broke upon his ear, and a laugh rang out merrily from behind the bushes of the pleasure-ground. The next moment Judy and Dick came into sight, followed by a couple of the garden lads bearing a wicker basket and various mysterious packages. They were turning away to the

right, when Judy suddenly waved her hand
and stood still.

"You have come just in the nick of time!"
she cried to Hugh. "Maud is sketching down
by the lake to-day, so I suggested we should
take our tea there and join her."

"We waited till the last moment, thinking
you would turn up," said Dick. "I believe it
is past five now, and she will be abusing us
roundly."

Hugh silently wondered why people should
go out of their way to make their meals uncomfortable as a form of pleasure. A picnic,
when it was the excuse for a party of friends
collecting together, was a more rational amusement; but when two or three people, who might
have a meal at home without any exertion, in
the most perfect comfort, chose instead to give
themselves considerable trouble to make that
meal the essence of discomfort, where was the
sense of it? However, he was distinctly thirsty,
and as tea was not, after all, awaiting him on
the lawn, he must needs follow where he saw

some hope of obtaining it. Therefore, struggling to look amiable, he turned back with his cousins, and they hastened across the long grass, followed by the two lads, who could be heard indulging in suppressed giggles at intervals, as though they looked upon the proceeding in the light of a good but extremely foolish joke.

They soon found the place where Maud had established herself—a grassy promontory which jutted out into the lake, and was only joined to the bank by a narrow strip of turf, bricked on either side to protect it from the wear of the water. At a little distance up the lake was an old boat-house, with thatched roof and dilapidated, moss-grown pillars, which formed the subject of her sketch; and already it stood out clear and fresh upon her canvas, with the delicate tint of its velvet-gold moss faithfully reproduced, and the pale streaks of grey and pink lichen dotted with trembling scarlet cups. The still waters of the lake formed a foreground; beyond, was a rugged sweep of hill with a clump of feathery sunlit birches.

Judy and Dick, with the help of the two lads, collected some sticks, and proceeded to make a fire, which at first absolutely refused to burn, then instantaneously blazed into a crackling furnace, appalling to behold on a hot afternoon, and the flames of which, blown erratically hither and thither by the wind, filled the place with a cloud of smoke and ashes. Hugh did his best to assist in laying the cloth, and lifted plates, spoons, and cups aimlessly out of the basket at intervals. At the end of half an hour he was rewarded by a weak cup of tea, strongly flavoured with smoke, and bearing on its surface the corpses of two small flies, a spider, and a lanky black creature with many legs. He removed the corpses with a blade of grass, and drank off the contents of the cup hurriedly, for fear of fresh tragedies taking place in its creamy depths. Then, not feeling eager to avail himself of Judy's pressing offer of a second cup, he helped himself to some gooseberries, and sat lazily dropping the empty skins into the water, and watching them float away.

Judy's tea, on the contrary, seemed inter-
minable. She appeared to be enjoying herself
greatly. She laughed incessantly, made endless
quaint remarks, and kept up a volley of repartee
with Dick. Hugh, all unconsciously, began to
feel nettled at the slight share of attention
which she vouchsafed him. Only twice did she
address him, and then it was to deliver herself
of little sarcastic speeches which annoyed him.
For the most part she ignored his presence,
reserving all her conversation for Dick. Watching her with a mild sense of irritation, he
noticed that she had a faint soft colour in her
cheeks—caused either by excitement or by her
face having been scorched with the fire—but it
made her look younger and less wizened. Once
or twice he caught some likeness to the child-
face he remembered, but all such resemblance
was still of the nature of a caricature, and as
such was painful to him. He preferred to think
of what he silently termed the Judy of To-day as
a being wholly apart from that haunting vision
of what had once lived and been dear to him.

" Judy," remarked Dick, " what a gossip you
and Maud were having the other evening ! I
heard you through the wall, and marvelled at
the activity of your tongues. Why is it that
girls invariably make such a parade of being
tired and anxious to get off to bed, merely that
they may make their escape from the drawing-
room, and sit up half the night chattering in
each other's rooms ? "

" We have no smoking-room," said Judy,
acidly.

Dick tried to ignore this little thrust.

" Whenever," he continued, " I hear two
girls talking earnestly together, I know they
are discussing one of two subjects—a man or
a dress ! "

" Most superficial topics, certainly," retorted
Judy ; " but at least refreshingly non-personal !
Man, I have observed, has two subjects on which
he also can talk earnestly, but they are merely—
himself or his dinner ! "

She drained her tea-cup, looking gravely at
Dick over the brim.

"I hope we did not disturb you if you had gone to your room to write," observed Maud. "How is the book getting on?"

"Fairly well," Dick replied. "This heat isn't conducive to flights of genius—not that that perturbs me, as I have far greater faith in luck than genius any day; and as to reviews, Judy would tell you that their purport—always presuming the critic is a man—depends solely on whether he happens to write them before or after dinner."

"And if after," put in Judy, "whether the dinner was strictly satisfactory!"

"Why don't *you* write a novel?" said Dick. "I feel sure it would be a most remarkable production. Only what a bad time we unfortunate men would have!"

"That is rather a good suggestion," answered Judy, thoughtfully. "I might endeavour to show Woman in her true light. Novelists always pretend there is no medium in Woman's nature between loving and loathing. Improving novels describe the ' loving' (*entendu* between

those whose duty it is to love), questionable
novels describe the 'loathing' (given the same
conditions). I should portray the real state of
affairs—how marvellously little is your power
to affect us at all! Fancy taking the trouble
to love or loathe any male biped!"

"But you must describe both sides of the
case," said Dick, throwing a flat pebble along
the water. "For instance, when a man is in
love, I acknowledge he fancies it is the whole
of life; but, with his usual common sense, he
very quickly recognizes it was the faintest
ripple which stirred the surface of life's
stream——"

"Very poetical, and very true!" interrupted
Judy, ironically; "and the ripples in your life
used to succeed each other with such startling
rapidity!" She waved the cake-knife tragically.
"Though the wind which occasioned them blew
everlastingly from some new quarter, yet it
kept the water in one perpetual ferment! Now,
with us—to give you a more solid simile—I
assure you we look upon you as insignificant

links in life's machinery, of whose existence we
are just sufficiently conscious—from the height
of our sublime indifference—to show you the
forbearance a superior nature should always
exercise towards an inferior."

"Good gracious!" exclaimed Dick. "In
short, a mere case of *noblesse oblige*? May I
ask, is that why women so readily consent to
'love, honour, and obey' their inferiors?"

"Yes," answered Judy, imperturbably; "it is
a question of sheer politeness. Woman knows
that Man, in reality, will always obey her without having wit to discover the fact, and it would
be a pity to dispel all his little delusions!"

She laughed gaily, as she cut a great hunch
of cake and held it towards Dick as a peace-
offering.

Hugh looked at her with curiosity.

"I quite envy that girl," he said to himself.
"I wish that having tea under a different tree
to what I usually have it under could put me
into such spirits."

He rose up and wandered to the other side

of the promontory. A boat was moored to the bank there. He stepped into it, and, lying down, stretched himself out, and rested his head against one of the cushions. It felt very peaceful. He drew a pipe out of his pocket, lit it, and began puffing with sleepy contentment.

The air had grown cooler now. Overhead there was still a filmy whirring company of gnats and flies, but low down, near the water, the breeze had driven them away. The park was gold with waning sunlight; on the distant hills lay a blue shade. The long branches of the trees swung now into the sunlight, now into the shadow. The water, ruffled by a faint wind, lapped the side of the boat and rocked it noiselessly against the bank.

He lay listening to the confused murmur of voices the other side of the promontory. Now and then he could hear some remark of Judy's, or was startled by her little shrill laugh. Once he fancied that Dick announced an intention of going shooting. At intervals a fish rose out of the water with a gleam of silver scales and a cool soft splash. Later, a water-rat ran out of its hole in the bank and sent keen shimmering ripples far across the lake. Slowly he saw the shadow on the hills become purple, and grow a vague dim rose.

Then he must have fallen asleep, for it was with a start that he opened his eyes to discover his pipe had dropped down into the bottom of the boat, and the tobacco had fallen out. His first care was to brush the ashes off his coat; next he noted that the sun had grown a red-gold, and the sky was dyed with vivid streaks of crimson, green, and lemon. He began wondering sleepily what had roused him. The voices to which he had been listening seemed to have grown louder now. It must have been this which had disturbed his slumbers. What was going on? Curiosity overcame his drowsiness; he raised himself on his elbow and peered over the bank.

Maud, kneeling on the grass, was packing up her sketching things. Judy, with a long branch

in her **hand, was** stooping over the bright sheet
of water, **trying to draw a** broad-leafed yellow
lily towards **her. Dick** had disappeared. To
the left, **where the fire** had been, lay **a** heap of
grey ashes; near them—Hugh looked again—
stood a figure which was unfamiliar to him.

With sleepy surprise, he studied this latter.
All which was presented to his **view was a** long
tweed **cloak, a coil of pale** gold **hair,** a tiny red
cap resting **somewhat** crookedly above the pale
coil. His present **view of the** cloak, he **told**
himself, was unprepossessing, and suggested
dowdy **middle-age**; but the shining hair, and
the space of soft **white neck** on which it lay,
gave **a** direct contradiction to this impression.
He decided the evidence of the neck must be
reliable.

Now fully **awake, still raising himself** on his
elbow, he watched for the moment when the
Unknown should turn and reveal more of her
personality. From under her skirts came a
small neatly-shod **foot;** it poked the powdery
sticks on the ground and stirred them till a

few dying sparks sprang from their midst, then it patted them down reprovingly. The interest was increasing. Next the breeze from the water blew back the tweed cloak, and revealed the folds of a blue cotton dress and a fluttering white ribbon.

Now the owner of the cotton dress and tweed cloak had moved towards the basket in which reposed the tea-things, apparently with the intention of choosing a pear from some fruit which lay upon the folded cloth. Maud, on the other hand, shading her eyes, was gazing at the boat-house as though noting regretfully that it looked more picturesque in the present light than when she had sketched it ; soon she rose to her feet.

" Aline ! " she called, " it is getting late."

' Aline ' ? Where had Hugh lately heard the name ? With a flash of recollection there came back to him the scene in the churchyard—Judy's dust-coloured figure leaning against the dazzling white cross, the gleaming letters, the sleepy sunshine, the oppressive stillness. He could

almost hear the quick enthusiastic tones—" She
had hair like thick shimmering gold, a face like
a wild rose, and great violet eyes with long
curling lashes." They had described another
Aline, the tale of whose brief life had ended
in a tragedy at which he had laughed. Had
the other Aline been like the girl before him—
just so fair, so young, so bright-eyed, before the
shadow came which wrecked her life?

In after-years Hugh dwelt on his thoughts at
this moment with a belief that it was more than
the apparently chance likeness of names which
brought back to his mind with insistence a tale
to which, at the time of telling, he had given
but casual attention. Yet, in point of fact, it
was with a brain wholly free from presentiments
that he then noted how the girl before him
tallied with, and surpassed, Judy's description
of her ill-starred namesake; how the heavy
cloak fell back from her slight, daintily-clad
figure; how long curling lashes veiled two
blue eyes, then lay, soft and dark, on two pink
cheeks; how the red-gold light of sunset

wrapped her about, and the leaves, quivering overhead in a fiery glow, let tremulous waves of colour wander over her fair hair and glad young face.

It was an exquisite picture—the blue figure against the space of angry sky, the dancing leaves, the sheet of flame-coloured waters paling to shades of orange and rose.

Softly Hugh pulled the boat against the bank, and stepped out upon the grass. No one observed him; he gave a short cough, and Judy's quick ears alone caught the sound.

" Goodness ! " she exclaimed, looking round. " So you have woke up at last ! I thought there had been a suspicious absence of snoring from your direction for the last ten minutes ! "

It was scarcely the introduction which Hugh could have wished. He had some difficulty in hiding his annoyance. Maud laughed. The girl, pausing in the act of biting a big golden pear, turned to look at him.

Elle s'habille.
Elle babille.
Elle se déshabille.

CHAPTER VII.

ON nearer view Hugh decided she might be a year or two older than he had at first supposed. Her face had a childish softness and roundness, but it had also a piquancy of expression which lent it more definite charm. Her eyes were very dark, with an unusual brilliancy of colouring.

Maud came forward.

"Hugh," she said, "I think you have heard us speak of Miss Graham?"

So this was Judy's companion—the distant cousin she had told him came to live with her after he went abroad. And he had fancied her old, and asked if she were like Fräulein Stutz!

The girl had stepped nearer.

" I don't think we have met before," she observed shyly, lifting her eyes to his face. " I never came to Lilcot till after you had left for India."

The soft colour in her face had deepened, her eyes were hidden by the long dark lashes.

Hugh grasped the little brown hand which was being held towards him.

" How stupid of me not to guess who you were!" he said cordially. "The fact of the matter is, I was told you were not expected till to-morrow; so, you see, I was utterly unprepared for my present good fortune."

" How pretty!" commented Judy from her post of observation near the lake. "Hugh never aired such exquisitely turned phrases for our benefit, Nellie!"

Miss Aline Graham—or Nellie, as she seemed also called—took this interruption with smiling good-humour.

" In that case I must consider myself highly

honoured!" she said prettily, looking up at
Hugh with a smile. "You see, Judy does not
appreciate her good fortune." And she then
proceeded to explain that, having found the
Daltons, with whom she had been staying,
were obliged to leave home for a visit a day
earlier than they had expected, she had felt
afraid she might be in the way if she remained
longer, so had telegraphed for the carriage to
meet her at the station, and had come over by
an afternoon train. Then, hearing Maud and
Judy were down by the lake, she at once set
off to look for them.

"I am afraid you must have arrived too
late for any tea," said Hugh, glancing in the
direction of the large basket. "It seems to be
all packed away."

"Oh, but she has been here some time," put
in Judy, still balancing herself perilously far
over the water. "You forget you have been
asleep! We went to look at you once or
twice, and you have no idea how sweet and
innocent you looked with your head on that

dark-green cushion! Nellie was quite fascinated. She thought it a pity you were not hung round with picturesque art muslins!"

A sudden shadow passed over Aline Graham's bright face.

"Don't invent in this absurd manner, Judy!" she said angrily.

"There, I have caught it at last!" remarked Judy, placidly drawing the broken lily towards her. Whether her observation referred to the flower or to Aline's wrath was left to the imagination.

At this juncture Maud stretched herself wearily.

"We really must be going home," she said. "I shall leave my sketching things here with the basket for the servants to bring up."

Judy came up the bank placing the wet lily triumphantly in her belt. The flower which had been so graceful floating on the water looked stiff and ungainly in its present position, but she appeared supremely satisfied with its effect; and, after giving a glance round to make sure none of the tea-things had been overlooked and left lying on the grass, now announced her willingness to start.

" Won't you be very hot walking up in that cloak, Miss Graham?" asked Hugh, with a lurking desire to see the pretty little figure beside him to better advantage.

" No ! " Aline shook her fair head so that the scarlet cap slipped further on one side. " I really could not burden you with it. It was horridly foolish of me to come in it, but I started off here directly I arrived, and did not discover I was too hot till I was some way from the house."

" That being so, I shall insist upon your letting me have it," said Hugh; and as he moved nearer to lift it off her shoulders, she yielded with a faint show of resistance.

As they strolled from the promontory he did not regret his little manœuvre. Although he had a particular dislike to having his arms encumbered with either parcels or wraps, it

was worth so slight a penalty to see the girl
beside him unfettered in her movements.
Relieved to be rid of the heavy cloak, she trod
through the grass with a light swinging step.
Her blue dress fell about her in clinging folds ;
he noted its neatness and the perfection with
which it fitted her slight figure. A white
ribbon which served her as a belt seemed to
accentuate the slimness of her waist.

Maud and Judy followed more slowly. The
former was tired after her long afternoon's
work in the fresh air ; the latter had effervesced
her overflow of spirits, and seemed disinclined
to talk. As they turned up the park in silence,
the pair in front were already some way ahead.
They could see Aline was talking with great
animation, and from time to time gesticulating
with her little sunburnt hands. Hugh was
looking down at her with an amused smile.
The sunset bathed them both in its orange
glow, and tinted her dress a curious pink,
which quivered back into blue as his shadow
fell across it.

Judy tried to move the lily in her belt; its stem broke; she plucked it out with evident irritation and flung it away.

Maud looked back half-pityingly at the golden cup-shaped blossom left to die, with its wet leaves smothered in dust.

"So like you," she said, "to spend all that trouble in getting what you throw away at once!"

"Why like me?" asked Judy, with a note of sharpness in her voice. "To most people the spice of life lies in pursuit, not possession."

Maud did not betray any amusement at the little sententious speech. Her slow dreamy gaze followed the direction of Judy's eyes, and rested on the pair in front. After a lengthened pause she spoke.

"Nellie Graham gets prettier each time I see her," she said thoughtfully.

The two figures in the distance seemed veiled in thin fire. The grass over which they stepped had been burnt by the sun into tufts of a dull maize hue, and caught the red light palely. They were walking more swiftly now, but not in a direct line for the house. Perhaps Aline was too absorbed in her conversation to notice the long curve she was taking out of her way.

"Maud," remarked Judy suddenly, "you used to be very pretty."

"Thank you," answered Maud, " for the implied hint that I am very much the reverse at present. Well——"

"No, you are not pretty," asserted Judy; "you are handsome. You are a big striking creature people would always notice and admire. There is something grand about you—the way you carry yourself, the set of your head, your quiet apathetic manner. But no one could call you pretty. It does not apply to you now. Once upon a time it did. You were a slim willowy thing, with a brilliant complexion and sparkling mischievous eyes. I used to think you bewitching."

"What is all this à propos of?" asked Maud. "I have grown fat now, and a few extra pounds of flesh alter one's views of life mysteriously."

"Well, in the days when you were minus those extra pounds which oppress you—in the days, say, when you became engaged to Hubert Cox—how used you to feel when you were talking to men?"

A faint smile flickered over Maud's face, but she suppressed it. She looked again at the figures in the distance.

"You want me to analyse my nature in that vanished past when I was pretty—is that it?"

"Did the fact of men's presence always make you perk up?" asked Judy, earnestly. "Did you feel an odd excitement, a craving to make yourself fascinating that they might love you?"

"Let me see," said Maud, gravely. "As a staid elderly matron I have learnt to look upon men as impossible creatures to excite one's self about; but in old days a man certainly had an odd inexplicable interest attached to him.

There is a curious fascination in flirting.   It is a kind of mental fencing."

"Then you used to want every man to be in love with you?"—with an expression of keen interest.

"Pah!   No!" exclaimed Maud, a slight contempt thinning her straight lip. "I don't know anything in the world so obnoxious as having some being in love with one whom one cannot care for. All the poetry of love vanishes when it strikes no responsive chord in one's own heart. Looking on at it, cold and sane, one sees it only under its foolish or its brutish aspect; it brings a sense of amusement or disgust. I often think how strange it is that, to a pure-minded woman, the kiss of one man means what is exquisite and entrancing, and the kiss of any other would bring such a sense of sickening degradation."

Judy smiled a little satirical smile.

"If love is so obnoxious, flirting may be described as slaving to get the last thing in the world you wish to have," she said dryly.

"No," answered Maud; "it might more often be described as human nature asserting itself unawares." The sun, a ball of fierce red, dazzled her eyes. She opened her parasol and held it slanting over her head, so that the blue shade cast an unwonted pallor over her clear dark skin. "I used to make myself pleasant to men all-innocently. There was an undefined glamour of romance over the proceeding, a sense of the Might-be which lent it its fascination; but this I only dimly understood. I wanted to be liked; I never wanted to be loved. My girlish affection for Hubert Cox grew from the fact that he let me enjoy his appreciation of me quietly, and never frightened me by any display of passion. In every woman's nature exists the innate desire to be admired and liked, but the pleasure of exciting love as an amusement can appeal only to low natures."

"Then," queried Judy, "you would consider Nellie a low nature because she flirted with that wretched little curate at Ilworth for the sheer fun of making him propose?"

"What, that little Mr. Todd?" said Maud, an irrepressible wave of merriment breaking over her face. "Poor little man! Why is it that, to onlookers, the ridiculousness or the poetry of love is entirely a matter of personal appearance? I can't help wanting to laugh at the notion of Mr. Todd in love; if he were six foot and good-looking, I might see all the romance or pathos of the situation." She checked herself abruptly. "I should say it was contemptible of Nellie," she answered; "but low——! My dear Judy, you are an *enfant terrible* in the way you digest and apply one's remarks! I don't think poor Nellie a low nature. She gives way to the natural craving of a pretty girl for admiration, and it has had the inevitable result of blunting any keen sensitiveness to the feelings of others. As a matter of fact, we never indulge in any amusement at the expense of a fellow-creature without its reacting twofold on our own souls. Nellie is shallow, empty-headed, and perhaps making herself empty-hearted; but, so far, there is no pronounced harm in her."

They turned into the grounds. Here the bushes cast broad still shadows across the pink-hued grass, and the yews were sharply black in a solemn twilight. The long branches of an araucaria stirring slowly looked like a gigantic octopus.

They trod more wearily as their feet sank with stealthy silence into the cool moss. A bird flew, shrieking noisily, from one great tree to another. A white rabbit, which had been nibbling the grass, scampered away and sat alert, with its long ears listening and a keen anxiety on its face. Judy tried to coax it into friendliness, and it hopped slowly from her as she approached, twitching its fine white whiskers nervously, and looking back out of the corner of its eyes with a grave distrust. Further on, they were greeted by a tremulous wave of delicate scents from the flower-beds in the front of the house, and the vivid sky again showed beyond a line of spiky black rhododendron leaves.

When they reached the wide open lawn, they

seemed stepping out of an uncertain twilight back into the glare of a red day. Judy climbed slowly on to the topmost terrace and paused. The park looked ablaze with the flames of an invisible furnace. The houses of the village were dusky blue against a blood-red sky. On the left a grey veil had stolen over the heavens, in which showed the globe of a thin nebulous moon.

"I like to picture how this will look in spring," said Maud, half closing her eyes, "when the tall poplars are a network of pale nodding buds, and the pink blossoms of the almond trees are like tinted foam against the sea-blue of the sky. Everything is scorched and weary now."

"Next spring I mean to have these beds all gold with daffodils," said Judy, thoughtfully.

A moment later she turned quickly to Maud.

"What are you looking at now?" she asked suspiciously.

"To answer you I must make a personal remark."

" Make it ! "   Judy was biting her lip.

" I was thinking, then," said Maud, slowly,
" what a strange face you have, Judy ! One
half of it is a direct contradiction to the other
half.   Your eyes flatly contradict your mouth.
Your mouth tells your surface-self; it is defiant,
self-contained, cynical—a trifle bitter.   Your
eyes read deeper into your soul—they are grand
eyes ; there is strength and truth and softness
in them ; I read all sorts of fine possibilities
there !   If "—and her voice assumed a gentle
earnestness—" I could read in my own eyes
half the nobility of soul I see in yours, I should
be well content, Judy."

Aline, coming briskly up the park, paused to
look at the view.

" This is a dear old place ! " she said.   " I
love Lilcot ! "

" And yet," said Hugh, " I hear there is some
talk of your wanting to leave it ? "

She brushed back a loose lock of hair which
had blown into her eyes.

" My aunt is very anxious I should go and live with her after Christmas. You see, I always spent all my holidays there as a child, so it is really my first home, and I was very fond of Edinburgh. I have not yet heard what Uncle Edward thinks I had better decide to do. For some things I don't at all want to leave here, for others I do. Sometimes it is very solitary. Judy is not much of a companion, you see, and she never cares about going to any of the garden-parties or little amusements one might get. Then, too—you won't mind my saying so?—she is peculiar and a little difficult to get on with. They tell me, too "—she looked at him questioningly—" that you are coming to live at home soon, and that will make a difference."

" What difference would it make ? " asked Hugh, looking at her intently.

Again her eyes drooped and the soft colour on her cheeks deepened swiftly. She hesitated.

" I should feel I was no longer needed," she said, with a shade of embarrassment.

Hugh did not remove his gaze from her face.

" You don't think it might be unkind of you
to leave me to the same solitude?" he asked,
half jestingly.

She was very pretty, with her hair all ruffled
by the breeze, and the soft glowing light on
her face.

They had reached the terrace in front of the
house, where, a moment before, Maud and Judy
had been standing. Now no one was in sight.
She moved a few paces, then paused near one
of the open French windows, and stood playing
with the handle, rubbing it backwards and
forwards till it grew bright beneath her touch.

" You wish to go because you think my
presence would make Lilcot less pleasant?"
said Hugh, smiling.

Aline lifted her eyes slowly and looked at
him.

" No," she said at length, " I thought I should
be in the way. That was why."

There was a witchery in the evening light,
the stillness, the girl's soft face.

" Do you think so still ?" whispered Hugh.

But Aline was gone.

The hall clock was striking eight. It was ten minutes fast, and that meant ten minutes only to dress for dinner. Before Hugh could realize her absence, she was running lightly up the oak staircase with a smile upon her lips. Gaining her room with all speed, she closed the door, and, hastening to the wardrobe, drew from thence a red silk evening-dress, which she flung in readiness upon the bed. Next she walked to her dressing-table in the window, and stopped before the tall looking-glass to remove her hat. The wood round the glass framed her reflection like a picture. She paused and studied it critically.

Her fair hair was all disordered. Her scarlet cap was on one side. It looked picturesque so. The brightness of its colour made her skin transparently white; the pink of her cheeks was heightened by contrast. Now she lifted up a hand-glass and turned her dainty little head sideways. The knot of hair gleamed like gold where it rested on the soft neck, a few stray locks curled round her tiny pink ears; she could see the soft bloom upon her cheeks, and the curve of the long dark lashes which brushed them lightly as she bent her gaze downwards. She laid the glass down and leant towards the soft dimpling face which approached her own. The red pouting lips were very close. With a not very original impulse of self-appreciation, she bent to kiss them, then started slightly at the cold contact of the glass. Next, she wound her arms round the framework. Her eyes sparkled and laughed back to their own reflection.

"You *dear* thing!" she said. "If I were a man, you are the only girl I should ever care to look at!"

END OF VOL. I.

PRINTED BY WILLIAM CLOWES AND SONS, LIMITED,
LONDON AND BECCLES.